Melissa's Viking

Melissa's Viking

Lisa Smelter

gatekeeper press™
Columbus, Ohio

Melissa's Viking

Published by Gatekeeper Press
2167 Stringtown Rd, Suite 109
Columbus, OH 43123-2989
www.GatekeeperPress.com

Library of Congress Control Number: 2022938658

ISBN (hardcover): 9781662922084
ISBN (paperback): 9781662922091
eISBN: 9781662922107

CHAPTER
ONE

Each of the Hillman siblings earned their college degrees in business. In this way, they took after their father, Roy. Mark, the eldest, had his Doctorate in Business Administration and had been a professor at a New York college before moving back to Litton to become director of several shelters. Matthew, the second son, had his master's degree in International Business, with an emphasis on foreign languages, and now worked at the Litton Airport. Melissa, the only girl, and the baby of the family had her bachelor's degree in business. She was greatly interested in managing a small store—be it grocery, clothing, or some other kind of retail store.

She hadn't known what to major in when she started college. Her parents encouraged her to start out with an open mind and see what interested her the most as a result of taking a large variety of college classes. At the outset, she thought that she wanted to major in either environmental science or business.

The young professor in her first business class was so dynamic that she subsequently developed an interest in, and enjoyed learning about, the business field. She knew that she would always be interested in all things related to the environment, but running a business, such as a store, was what she finally decided to focus on in her studies.

Melissa had always been a dreamer. When she was small, she loved the fantastical life of princesses and knights. She loved the feminine flowing dresses and tiaras worn by the women of the Middle Ages. Because she was the only girl in her entire family, she was a pampered little princess. Both sets of grandparents indulged her by buying every pretty princess outfit they could find. Her parents sweetly accepted, and even encouraged, her love for anything to do with fairytales.

Only her brothers had been disdainful of her and her love for such things. She had always wanted their acceptance and approval, but she could tell by their rolling eyes and teasing that they wished she was a boy. Finally, when she was around ten, she gave up her pretty gowns and enchantments and allowed her brothers to teach her how to play the sports they liked. She did it to gain their love and approval.

Mark was ten years older than she was and already in college, so he only played with her when he was teaching her how to shoot baskets or play softball. Matt was five years older than she was and still in high school. He treated her the same way as Mark did. By the time Mark moved to New York when she was twelve, she started to enjoy playing sports with them. She missed Mark when he left, but she thought, realistically, that he probably never gave her another thought. Matt still played ball with her until he went to live in Europe while he was in his second year in college.

Melissa had always been tall. As a little girl, she was usually taller than her little friends. She came from a tall family. Everyone on both sides of her family was tall. Her mom was nearly five feet eleven inches tall, and both grandmothers were statuesque, so she thought, with reluctant acceptance, that she would be tall, too.

She shot up five inches in one year when she was thirteen. At that point, she was five feet eight inches tall. She was even taller than many of the boys in her class. Now, at twenty-seven, she was five feet ten inches tall.

Roy and Kay's youngest was a kind and pleasant young woman. She had a nice sense of humor and could get along with just about anyone. Her face had a gentle kind of beauty. Her long glossy dark curly hair surrounded her heart-shaped face. Her mouth curved sweetly, and her blue eyes were lovely, with their long and thick dark lashes. She had a nice figure. When she smiled, her whole face lit up, and she looked very pretty. However, when she frowned or looked sad, her pleasant face looked quite ordinary.

Melissa had been working these last few years as an assistant manager at one of the big department stores in town, but she wanted a greater challenge. She scoured the internet and papers for possible jobs in which she would be able to start as the manager and supervise her own staff. She was generally thought of as a calm and quiet young woman, but she had a firm determination and had learned how to manage subordinates with fairness and competency.

She interviewed for as many jobs as she could, but all too often the interviewer determined that her demeanor was too sweet and demure to be that of a store manager. It was a problem, to be sure. She tried pulling her hair back into a severe bun and wearing a no-nonsense suit, but somehow, she just ended up looking like a little girl in grown-up clothes. Melissa concluded that it was her heart-shaped face and gentle mouth that caused her to look so incapable of taking care of store employee discipline.

The people who knew her well understood that she could be quite firm and even haughty when she needed to be. But mostly, she was a happy young lady with a warm smile and a loving personality. She had a few very good friends and now got along well with her family. Her brothers sometimes teased her until she could stand no more—then lookout! If she felt that someone was doubtful of her abilities, she could cut them down to size in a New York minute. The victim usually did not have a clue that she could be that strong and abrupt, although most people never saw that side of her. Having two older brothers, she grew up tougher than she looked on the outside.

Finally, one day in late spring, Melissa interviewed for the position of general manager at a smaller grocery store. It was not a franchised store, but a one-of-a-kind store, owned by two bachelor brothers. Thomas and Timothy Olson, identical twins, already in their late sixties, wanted a young manager who would hopefully stay for a good long time.

The Olsons were looking for a manager who could use technology to better track inventory and yet also possessed necessary interpersonal skills to effectively manage the staff. They had no idea how to even turn on the computer that sat unused and dusty on the end table in the staff lounge. Their business was starting to fail because they were unable and unwilling to put in the time to keep themselves afloat. They needed someone to track the inventory, buy new products, cease the pilfering from the staff, and basically do anything to keep the store going. They were tired and sometimes wanted to throw in the towel. However, they were willing to give it one last chance.

Melissa's resume seemed too good to be true. They invited her to come into the store, look around, and then participate in an interview. Melissa arrived at the meeting wearing her blue power suit and having her hair neatly controlled in a French pleat. She surveyed the store, including the back storeroom. She walked around, silently taking note of the products and their prices, and spoke with a few of the cashiers. Almost immediately, she knew what the problems were at Tollie's Grocery Store.

When the brothers brought her into the staff lounge to interview her, Melissa asked them if they had a private room where they could speak. There were several employees sitting in the lounge having their lunch. The brothers looked very surprised and a bit upset that Melissa did not want to talk in front of the other employees. She smiled and told them that she had some confidential information that she wanted to share with them that she did not want to talk about in front of anyone else. They looked at each other and shrugged. They took her into an old office that had a scratched-up table and a few wobbly chairs in it, but at least they were able to close the door for some privacy.

In the interview, Melissa introduced the concept of using the computer and some good bookkeeping applications to track inventory, prices, and sales. She told them that they had a large surplus of certain groceries that did not sell very well for some reason. There was too much waste, as well. Some products had to be thrown out because they expired before they could be sold.

Several cashiers mentioned to her that the store always had too many of certain products and that there were never enough of some products when they ran sales on them. Melissa talked confidently about how she could easily track the sales of all the products. She shared her plan of having a candid conversation with all employees about shoplifting and the overall problem of shrinkage.

The brothers were surprised but very pleased with the information that Melissa shared with them. After an hour of discussion, they offered her the job as manager. They had no idea what to pay her, but Melissa had done her homework and had a spreadsheet of the salaries of other managers in similar jobs.

Melissa guaranteed them a marked increase in store profit within six months if they gave her the freedom to put into practice the things she talked about. If she was unsuccessful in doing so, she would resign from the position.

The brothers did not want their life's work to go under, so they agreed with Melissa's suggestions. Melissa told them that she had to give a two-week notice at her current job but would start as their new manager in fifteen days. They agreed and shook her hand with relief and happiness.

Before she left them, she had to ask, "Why is the store named Tollie's Grocery Store?"

One of the brothers, Thomas, smiled widely and told her, "Well, our family name is Olson. Our friends always called us Ollie. Because our first names begin with a T (Thomas and Timothy), we stuck a T in front of Ollie to get Tollie. No one else ever had that name, as far as we know. So that made our little store truly unique. Clever, don't you think?" His blue eyes twinkled as he looked at Melissa.

She nodded, her eyes bright with laughter, "Yes, very clever. I would never have guessed that in a hundred years. But I like the name very much. I hope to make Tollie's a viable business for you for the rest of your lives. I will work very hard for you and the store. Thank you so much for the opportunity to show you that I can do it. I have so many ideas already. I will see you in two weeks, gentlemen," she told them. They shook hands again, and she left them still talking about the new changes she planned to make.

Melissa smiled as she drove home. She was pleased that the Olson brothers took her recommendations seriously. She knew that the power suit alone wouldn't win them over. The greatest pleasure came from the realization that she had solid ideas for successful retail management, and now she was going to be able to put them to work.

The smile remained on her face as she parked her car. She entered her comfortable apartment and looked around with quiet happiness. It was a great apartment and very comfortably furnished. Clarabelle, the tabby cat, met her by the door, weaving around Melissa's legs. She wanted her supper.

Melissa reached down and picked up Clarabelle, saying, "Hello, Puss, I'm home. What do you know? I finally got a job as a store manager! I'm going to start managing Tollie's Grocery Store in about two weeks. But first, I need to write out my resignation letter to hand in tomorrow. I just can't believe it. I finally got someone to take me seriously. I am going to be the best manager that any small business ever had."

She couldn't tell if Clarabelle was excited for her or simply intent on being fed. Deciding that it was a little of both, she swung the cat around and danced a few steps into the kitchen. She got Clarabelle's food out and then looked in her fridge for something for herself. Nothing looked enticing, so she called her neighbor and best friend, Brad, and asked him if he wanted to go in on a pizza with her.

Brad laughed and said, "Always, Melly. Our usual?"

Melissa smiled into the phone and said, "Yes, the usual. I'll order it. If you have any wine, bring it with you. I'm celebrating tonight."

Brad asked her, "What's the good news, Melly?"

Melissa laughed with pure happiness and said gleefully, "Brad, I got my first job as a manager of a store today. I'll tell you more about it when you come over, okay?"

"Sure, Melly. I will be there in half an hour. I'll look and see if I have any wine." He hung up the phone, and Melissa went into her bedroom to change her clothes.

As always, she pivoted around the room to take in the full effect. It was an old-fashioned-looking room that was decidedly feminine. Her brass four-poster queen-size bed gleamed in the overhead light. Its antique flowered quilt made the bed look so inviting. Her dark brown antique wardrobe and dressing table with its embroidery-covered chair were the perfect foil to the pale blue plush carpet. Her walls were covered with a sweet tiny flowered wallpaper. Wrought iron shelves filled with porcelain and small china animals covered her walls. The walls also sported large black cursive inspirational words. Her favorite word among the grouping was "Believe". She did believe in herself.

She scoured the local antique stores and flea markets to find her treasures. She just loved old wooden and black wrought iron decorations. Her living room was graced by similar antiques and homespun articles. She loved the overall look of her home. It was the one place that truly expressed her personality. She always tried to act so professional and practical at her jobs, but her home was her haven, and she loved giving it her personal touch.

As Melissa walked into her living room, she pulled her long curling dark hair back into a ponytail using a big pink scrunchy to hold it. She had at least a dozen different scrunchies—one to match every color that she wore. Tonight, she wore a soft pink sweater and blue jeans with her pink slippers.

She knew that Brad would probably tease her about her color-coordinated outfit, but she didn't care. She could dish it out as well as he could. She usually found plenty of things to tease him about. He was a dentist and was a tiny bit obsessive about brushing his teeth after every meal. She had teased him about that for years, ever since she had moved next door to him almost four years ago. She treated him like another of her brothers, and he accepted that just fine.

When they first met, he was in the throes of a love-hate relationship with a young woman named Bonnie. Melissa talked with him and helped him through their nasty break-up. They had been the best of friends ever since. They were too comfortable together to date each other, but they did find it handy to have someone to take to special events at times. Brad was the only person who knew about Melissa's passion to become a manager and make her own mark on the world. Even her family did not know how much it meant to her.

Melissa had been called Melly by her family since she was a toddler. Her elder brother, Mark, had started it. She loved the nickname when she was young. Her little school friends and even some of her teachers had called her that. When she got to the ripe old age of thirteen, she decided that the name Melly was too babyish for a teenager. She insisted that everyone call her Melissa. It was only after many arguments with her parents and brother, Matt, that she was consistently called Melissa.

Mark had already moved to New York by the time she was thirteen and saw her infrequently for many years after that. When he came back to live in Litton a few years ago, he automatically called her Melly, again. Melissa had decided to let him still call her that, for that was how he remembered her. It caught on again, and soon her whole family was calling her Melly. The only difference between now and when she was thirteen, was that now she was a confident young woman, and she realized that her family only used it as a term of endearment. It once again made them feel closer to her. Brad heard her family call her that so often that he fell into the habit of calling her Melly, as well. Only Melissa's nearest and dearest ever called her Melly, now.

TWO

Melissa started her new job at the grocery store. She came in with her plans all laid out on a few sheets of paper. The first thing she did was meet with the Olson brothers. She found them pathetically eager to do whatever she suggested. She stated that she would need an assistant manager because she could not work all the hours that the store was open. She suggested that she work forty hours a week and the assistant manager work thirty hours a week. She openly wondered if there were any current employees who might be a good assistant manager.

The Olsons gave her the names of several highly recommended employees who seemed to know quite a lot about the store and the merchandise. Melissa promised to interview them and determine if one of them was qualified and wanted to take the job. She explained that she needed a private office, even a very small one, where she could work privately. They agreed to fix up the little decrepit office for her use.

She planned to interview all the current employees to learn more about each of their jobs and to determine their work ethic. She told the Olsons that she would be changing the food order with their supplier. She explained that they were wasting good money by buying too much of some products and not enough of others. She took them around the store and showed them what she was talking about. They nodded their heads and agreed that there certainly was some waste going on. They said they trusted her and agreed to let her put her ideas into practice.

Melissa had only been there a few weeks when the food supplier was scheduled to come in and talk with her. She found out that his name was Erik Lundstrom and that he had been supplying Tollie's Grocery Store for three years. She was ready with her new order the day that he was scheduled to come in.

*   *   *

Erik walked into Tollie's with a jaded attitude. He had just spent several hours with an old client who wanted to change everything about his ordering process. Now, this afternoon, he was going to have to deal with a *new* manager at Tollie's. He wasn't looking forward to dealing with some *new* manager with *new* ideas. He had always dealt with the Olson brothers before. While he suspected that they ordered the wrong things for their small store, it was an easy account because the order remained the same each month. He had suggested other products to them over the years, but they continually refused to change their monthly order with him. After the day that he was having, he needed an easy transaction to turn things around and end on a positive note.

He waved to a few of the cashiers he was accustomed to seeing every month. They smiled back at him in acknowledgment. Erik was a tall, large, and muscular man with dark blond hair and light blue eyes. When he was not smiling, his strong square jaw and large grim mouth made him look exactly like a Viking from his Scandinavian ancestry. His suit coat looked like it could barely contain his physique. He felt more comfortable in worn jeans and either a flannel shirt or a sweatshirt. In fact, when he was dressed in his most comfortable clothes, he looked like he should be sailing on a Viking ship or chopping down magnificent trees in a forest somewhere.

He walked directly back to the familiar staff lounge where he expected to find the new manager. He knew her name—Melissa Hillman. He fleetingly wondered if she was related to Mark Hillman, who was the director of St. Mary's Shelter. Mark had ordered food from Erik ever since he had taken over as director. They were casual friends and sometimes played racquetball or basketball together.

He saw Melissa sitting there laughing gently while talking with one of the male cashiers. Even though he had sworn off women, Erik was immediately attracted to her gentle prettiness. He liked tall nicely shaped women. When she smiled, her whole face lit up. It was like seeing the sun come out on a gloomy day. He was quite frustrated with himself for being attracted to her. *Women were trouble with a capital T*, he quickly reminded himself.

Melissa saw him standing in the doorway looking at the cashier and herself. She murmured something quietly to the cashier, who got up and left the room, waving to Erik as he went. Erik went over to Melissa and held out his hand. "Ms. Hillman? I am Erik Lundstrom. I have an appointment with you to go over your grocery order."

Melissa smiled at him and shook his hand. *Here was a big man,* she thought. He looked just like a picture she had seen of a Viking from long ago. His deep slow voice matched his Viking persona. She was immediately attracted by his big tall blond looks. She grinned wider. "Yes, I'm Melissa Hillman. How do you do, Mr. Lundstrom? Please sit down. I'm afraid that we will have to use this room, as my office is still being redecorated."

Erik sat down at the table and brought out his clipboard with his usual order form for Tollie's. "Are you, by any chance, related to Mark Hillman, who is the director of St. Mary's Shelter?" he asked in a tolerantly friendly voice.

Melissa rolled her eyes but said quite cheerfully, "Yes, Mark is my elder brother. How do you know him?"

Erik explained, "He has ordered the Shelter's groceries from me ever since he took over there." Erik had to remind himself not to stare, which was becoming increasingly more difficult to do, as he was stricken by Melissa's beauty. He added, quickly, "He's a good man."

Melissa nodded and said, "Yes, he's great. Everyone likes Mark. Now, let's see if we can get this order figured out."

Erik anticipated no problems as he gestured to the order form. "The Olsons had a running order of the following products every month. I am sure that you will not want to change anything," he said with confidence.

"On the contrary, I *am* going to change many things, Mr. Lundstrom," she replied calmly.

Wait, did she just say 'change many things'? Erik thought to himself. *I was just beginning to like her!*

Erik looked surprised and then angry. "Why do you feel the need to change things, Ms. Hillman? The Olson's haven't changed anything in the three years that we have worked together," he said huffily. *Here goes my easy end of the day,* he thought with frustration.

Melissa just looked at him without expression and stated, "I know that, Mr. Lundstrom. That system has not been working for them.

They have a large surplus of certain products and not enough quantity of others. I can assure you that I have gone through all the inventory and have taken stock of the products in the store. My new order will help bring the store into better alignment. Now, here is my new order."

She held out her order form in front of him.

Erik did not know exactly why he had to blow up at her, but he snatched the order form from her hand and snarled, "Do you think that you know better than two men who have been running this store for forty years? You've had this job for what—two weeks? Why, you're nothing but a girl who is wet behind the ears. You look like a little girl who is playing at being a grown-up!"

Even Erik was surprised by what he had just said, but not by saying it. He was, indeed, frustrated.

All the unfounded stereotypes that she had ever endured made her see red. In a scathing voice, Melissa said, "You, sir, are unkind. I have no wish to talk with you again. I will email my order in from now on. Good day!" She turned on her heel and quickly walked away.

He looked after her with a ferocious frown. He liked to get in the last word but was not able to do that in this situation. She walked away too quickly. He realized that he had gone too far. He felt mad at himself. He did not want to be attracted to her after the nonsense he had gone through with Diane. If Ms. Hillman had been an older, less attractive woman, he would probably have been irritated but could have handled it. He involuntarily uttered a guttural sound through clenched teeth and thought, *my stupid attraction to her made me say those things!* He knew that he was going to have to apologize to her before next month's order. *Boy, this is just not my day,* he thought morosely.

After Mr. Lundstrom left the store, Melissa sat in the break room and thought about their conversation. She was still fuming. How dare he insult her! He didn't even know her. She knew that she overreacted a bit, but she was done with letting others call or think of her as a little girl in grown-up clothes.

She was a grown woman, and she knew what she was doing. She had spent quite a bit of time going over the inventory in the store and talking with the employees and customers. She knew that she had a good plan to help them turn the store around. She would do everything within her power to help the Olson brothers hang on to their store. It was their legacy.

She was just aching to get her teeth into this job and make it a big success. So now that big pompous man comes along to spout off his opinion that she wasn't mature enough to do the job correctly. Well, she would show him that he was way off base. She intended to cut him dead with a cold stare whenever she saw him.

Melissa was sure that he would come around to the store again. She would enjoy showing that irritating man that he was wrong about her. She would make him eat his words. With that final thought running around in her head, she took herself home for the day. When she got home, she let the beauty of her living room and Clarabelle sitting on her lap soothe her into a better frame of mind.

Erik made out the new order form for Tollie's Grocery Store on his computer. When he looked at the new order more closely, he could understand why Ms. Hillman made the changes. It made more sense for the size and location of the store. This store was in an established older quiet neighborhood. Most of the patrons were middle-income to low-income seniors and empty nesters. It made sense that they would want more of certain products and less of others. He realized that Ms. Hillman was correct in her decision to go with the new products.

He needed to get his apology set before he visited Tollie's next month. No matter what she had said, he would still drop by on his regular visit. She could send him her order, but he still planned to show up at the store. He was sorry that he lashed out at her. It was in no way her fault. *If only I didn't find her so attractive,* he thought with a regretful shake of his head.

* * *

It was a week after Erik first met Melissa Hillman. He had thought about her a great deal. Her lovely smile was always there, in the back of his head. He was annoyed by it, so he decided to get some exercise and join Mark Hillman at the weekly basketball game that he and his friend, Paul, ran for the youth from the Shelter. He played with them a few times in the past.

He got there at six o'clock to help them sweep the parking lot to get it ready for the game. There were already quite a few people there. He waved to some of the folks that he had previously met. A few of the boys who came to play every week saluted him. He grinned at them and saluted back.

Smiling, he looked around him. He saw Melissa Hillman talking with her brother. She was laughing at him and smiling that lovely smile. Erik looked intently at her face. Her blue eyes were twinkling, and her whole face was lit up. She looked quite beautiful to him at that moment.

He walked over to talk with them. When Melissa caught sight of him, the smile slid right off her face. Her eyes, as well as the rest of her face, became shuttered. He was shocked at the difference between her happy face and her expressionless face. Melissa hugged her brother goodbye, looked sharply away from Erik, and walked quickly away.

Erik felt like a heel. Ms. Hillman obviously could not stand the sight of him. He knew that he absolutely had to apologize to her for that unfortunate conversation that they had when they first met. He watched her walk over to sit down next to some other women. He knew two of the ladies; one was Paul's wife, Sarah, and their young son. The other woman was Mark's wife, Susan. She appeared to be quite pregnant. A petite redhead and Melissa Hillman were laughing and whispering to each other.

Erik tried to look away, but there was just something so appealing about Melissa when she laughed or smiled. He did not want to like her. Given his experiences with Diane, he had enough of women for a while. With a great effort, he put her out of his thoughts and instead concentrated on playing basketball.

Melissa's eyes were drawn to Erik's big frame far too often. She hated him—why was she even watching him? It was like watching a tarantula walking up your arm. You knew it was not going to be a good thing, but you were powerless to stop watching it.

She had to admit to herself that he was good with the boys who were playing the game. He shouted encouragement to all of them and helped them whenever he could. *It must just be me that he dislikes*, she thought with sadness. Melissa was a girl who liked most people. She had a nice sense of humor and could get along with everyone. *Well, almost everyone,* she thought wryly.

When the game was over, Melissa decided to leave before the guys came over to pick up their wives. She usually enjoyed meeting up at one of their homes after the game, but Susan had told the group that Erik was coming over to talk about something with Mark. Melissa had no desire to see Erik Lundstrom up close or talk with him, so she said her goodbyes to the ladies before the men could walk over to them. She told them that she had a date and had to get going. She waved to her brothers and blew them a kiss before quickly walking to her car. She drove away without looking back.

Erik watched her go, a little frustrated. He thought that he might have the chance to speak to Melissa alone and apologize to her. Mark clapped him on the back and told him to come and meet everyone. Erik met Mark's brother, Matthew, and Matthew's new bride, Tessa. He became reacquainted with Susan and Sarah, as well.

Mark hugged his wife carefully and gently caressed her large tummy; then he dropped a kiss onto her stomach. He smiled sweetly at Susan and then asked her, "Hi, darling. Where did Melly go so quickly? I thought that she was coming over to our place tonight."

Susan's dimple flashed as she smiled at her husband. She shrugged and told him, "I thought so, too. But just before you guys walked over here, she told us that she had to go because she had a date. It's the first I heard of her having a date tonight."

Erik thought privately that Melissa probably left because she did not want to talk with him. It was too bad that he had been such a jerk to her at their first meeting. He didn't share any of his thoughts with the others. He agreed to follow them to Mark's house and talk.

Mark wanted to talk him into doing some volunteer work. Erik was pleased to do it. He knew that the Shelter was putting up a few homes and needed volunteers who knew their way around a hammer. It was the sort of volunteer work that Erik liked the best. He was a very physical guy and liked working outside with his hands.

They had a very pleasant time at Mark's, talking and laughing. He liked the women just fine, but only because they were already married. He tended not to trust young single women anymore. In his mind, he cursed Diane for putting him through so much stuff that he could hardly even look at a woman anymore without curling his lip in derision.

On Friday night, Melissa got a phone call from Mark. He told her about the project houses that the Shelter planned to build. He asked her if she would help them out the following day. Since it was one of the Saturdays that she did not have to work at Tollie's, she readily agreed.

"Mark, do you want me to ask Brad if he wants to volunteer, as well? I think he told me that he has this Saturday free," she asked him.

"Sure, bring Brad with you. Are you guys ever going to start dating?" Mark teased her.

"No, Mark, you know that Brad and I are just friends. He's like another brother to me—not that I need another one—what with you and Matt. He's my buddy, and he is a nice guy. One day I'm going to find the perfect woman for him," she retorted back at Mark.

Mark was serious for a second, "Melly, when are you going to find someone for yourself? Now that Matt and I are married, it's your turn to find love. What kind of man are you looking for? Maybe Susan and I can help find Mr. Right for you," he said with a ghost of a grin in his voice.

"Oh, no. I don't need you guys to try to find me a boyfriend. I'm not looking for anyone right now. I'm only twenty-seven. I've still got some time before I turn into an old lady, you know. Besides, if I start to get desperate, Brad will help me find someone. He has lots of male friends," Melissa stated emphatically.

"How about someone like Erik? You met him the other day. He might be just right for you," Mark asked in a serious voice.

"No way, I can't stand him!" Melissa said quickly and fiercely.

"Why not? You barely met him, Melly. How can you hate him already?" Mark was confused by her answer.

"I met him another time, and let's just say that his ugly true colors came out. So, a big NO. Don't try to fix me up with that guy. I'll never forgive you if you try to do that, Mark, and I mean that!" she said with some anger in her voice.

"Melly, I won't. Don't get so upset. Forget I even brought it up, okay? You will still come out to the project house tomorrow, right?" he asked her cajolingly.

"Yes, Mark, you can count on Brad and me to be there. Oh, and make sure you remember to bring some lunch this time. Remember last time we all did some volunteer work for the Shelter? You forgot to bring in any food. We were starving. And did you notice that no one volunteered for a long time after that?" she said with a bit of sarcasm in her voice.

"Don't worry, Melly. Susan has it all planned. She's much better at organizing than I am. Thanks, sis. See you tomorrow, then," Mark said.

CHAPTER

THREE

Erik started volunteering at the first project house that weekend. Mark, Paul, Matthew, their wives, and a few others were already there that Saturday morning. Mark had Erik help Matthew put together one of the sides of the house. Erik enjoyed the work because he was working with his hands outdoors, and because it distracted him from thoughts of Melissa.

Matt and he were engaged in general conversation when he saw Melissa arrive with a nice-looking young blond man. They were laughing together and teasing each other. Erik thought that this must be Melissa's boyfriend, for they seemed very close. He watched as Mark set them up painting something. From where he was working, he could hear her clear voice laughing at something that her partner said to her.

They had been working for half an hour when Melissa, standing straight to stretch her back, caught sight of Erik. Her laughing mouth suddenly became still, and she turned her back toward him. Then she said something to her friend, who, apparently amused, teased her and traded places with her so that she was working with her back to Erik. They all worked for another two hours before Mark called a halt for lunch.

He had a long table set up with submarine sandwiches, bags of chips, and cans of soft drinks. Erik held back to let everyone else choose their lunch before he picked out his own lunch. He watched Melissa take her boyfriend's arm and guide him through the line. She had a ready smile for everyone she spoke with. She never looked in Erik's direction at all. She and her friend took their lunch and went to a small picnic table that was located on the grass.

Erik got his lunch and looked around for Matt or Mark. They were sitting on the grass while their wives were sitting at another small table next to them. They waved him over. Erik lowered himself to the ground and started to eat. He could still see Melissa and her friend nearby at that picnic table.

Mark addressed Erik, "Hey, that is some great work you are doing. Do you think that you can come again next Saturday? We want to get as much done as we can while the weather is so nice."

Erik smiled at Mark and said in a friendly voice, "Sure, I like this kind of work. I have most weekends off. Unless I have something unexpected come up, you can count on me to help out."

"Thanks so much, Erik. We appreciate all the hard work you are doing. We definitely need your muscles," said Susan with a cheeky grin. Erik flashed a smile back at her.

"No problem, Susan. I'm glad to help," he told her. They all finished their lunch and got back to work. Erik watched Brad give Melissa a hand up, and they went back to work, as well.

After a few more hours of working non-stop, Mark called a halt. They were going to stop for the day. "Hey, everyone. Susan and I are treating all you wonderful workers to pizza at the Shelter this evening. Let me know if you plan to be there so we know how much pizza to order. We'll open the recreation center at

7:00 o'clock sharp. That way if any of you have other plans for the evening, you'll be done eating early," he told the crowd.

Erik hoped that Melissa would stop off for pizza. He was still bound and determined to get her by herself so that he could apologize. He watched Melissa and her friend walk over to Mark and talk with him. She smiled at Mark but shook her head no. She put her hand on her friend's arm and smiled at him, talking all the while. Mark frowned for a second, but it soon cleared, and he grinned at her. She gave him a big hug, waved to the others, and walked back to her car, arm in arm with her boyfriend.

Erik watched them go with no expression on his face. *Oh, well, there goes another chance to apologize,* he thought to himself. He allowed Mark to persuade him to come back to the Shelter for pizza. *I may as well go; I have nothing else to do tonight,* he thought.

They ended up having such a fun time. He was really starting to like Mark, Paul, Matt, and their wives, although he felt like the odd-one-out without a girl by his side. If he were truly honest with himself, he would admit that he missed having a girlfriend. He had had girlfriends by his side since he was seventeen years old. If only Diane had not made him lose his desire to be around young attractive single women. Well, that was his issue. He would just have to work through it.

Meanwhile, he needed to stop thinking about Melissa Hillman. It was blatantly clear to him that she cared nothing for him. She obviously loathed him. He would give anything to take back those unfounded and unkind words uttered to her in a few moments of frustration.

Mark called Melissa during the next week to see if she and Brad could volunteer at the project house again on Saturday. Melissa explained to him that she had to work from nine am until five pm at Tollie's Grocery Store every other Saturday. Matt and Tessa were planning to host a picnic supper for all the helpers starting about six o'clock. Melissa thought that she would be able to make it to Matt's house after work. She would stop off at her home first to change her clothes and then be there as soon as she could. Mark told her that he would let Matt and Tessa know.

That Saturday, Erik went back to the construction site with the regular gang. This time, Melissa did not show up to work with them. He overheard Mark telling Matt that Melissa had to work at Tollie's Grocery Store today. Apparently, she had to work every other Saturday until the store closed at five pm. Matt invited Erik to the picnic supper.

Erik went with them because they would not take no for an answer. They were often volunteering together and, as a result, spending hours upon end with each other. They were all becoming quite good friends. The band of happy workers had been at the picnic for about half an hour when Melissa showed up.

"Melly," shouted her brothers.

"I'm glad you could make it," said Matt. "Did you stop off and see Mom and Dad, yet? They were hoping to see you this weekend."

Melissa smiled at Matt and hugged him. "No, I told Mom that I would stop by for lunch tomorrow. I want to go to my church first. We have a special program going on this week at church, and I want to be there for it. Are you and Tessa going to go to Mom's, too?" She asked Matt.

"Yes, we'll be there, too. How was work today?" he asked her. They walked away, arm in arm, still talking. Erik could see Melissa stopping to talk with all her family and some of the other volunteers. She really looked quite adorable in her red shirt, black jeans, red sneakers, and a red scrunchy in her dark hair. Erik liked the way her curly hair swirled around in a bouncy ponytail.

A few minutes later, Melissa looked up and zeroed right in on Erik, who was sitting outside at the patio table. She frowned and turned away. Melissa kept well away from Erik all evening. She chatted in a friendly way with every other person there but kept at least twenty feet of distance between Erik and herself. She was one of the first to leave the gathering.

Erik kept an eye out for her the whole time she was there. How he wished that he could just go up to her and talk with her like everyone else. He could not stop thinking about her. Maybe if he had the chance to apologize, he could get her out of his system. *It would be like a cleansing,* he thought to himself.

Melissa went home after Matt's picnic and thought about Erik. He kept turning up wherever she went. She knew that her brothers liked him and would probably invite him to all their parties and get-togethers. Either she had to get over her dislike for him, or she would have to stop hanging out with her family so much.

That would be a pity because they had only been this close for the past few years—ever since Mark had moved back to Litton from New York and married Susan. Their mom couldn't believe how close they had all become.

Neither of her brothers, their wives included, would understand her antipathy toward Erik. She hadn't told her brothers about Erik's insulting words to her. Even if she had, they would probably not understand why she was so upset. They had told her those very same things in the past. No, if she could just continue to avoid him, she would be able to keep seeing her brothers at their special events.

She truly hoped that Erik wouldn't come into the store at the end of the month with his order form. She made sure that she sent him the email with her order well before the due date, so he wouldn't come looking for her in the store. Somehow, she thought that he would come in, anyway. He seemed like the type of man who liked to get his own way and to have the last word. Well, if that was the case, she would be ready for him. She did not intend to talk with him anytime soon.

*　*　*

That next Thursday night, Melissa stopped off at the Shelter to watch her brothers play basketball. She brought with her a toy truck for Paul and Sarah's little boy. Christopher was a year and a half old and the sweetest little boy that she had ever met.

Because Paul had been Mark's best friend for most of their lives, Melissa had grown up knowing him. He was a wonderful person. He had gently teased her all those years from the time she had been a tiny girl until the present time. She could even remember the time he rescued her from the big tree in the backyard. Mark and Matt had teased her into climbing it.

Mark had been very much the boss of the Hillman children. Melissa never felt like she fit in with her brothers because they were so much older than she was. When they dared her to climb the tree when she was six years old, she had gone for it. She wanted to prove to them that she wasn't just some silly little girl, so she climbed the tree. Once she was up in the branches, however, she was too scared to come down. She sat up there for a long time. Mark and Matt eventually forgot that she was up there. When they discovered that she was missing, everyone went looking for her in the backyard.

Paul had been at their house visiting Mark. He was the one who saw her way up in the branches. He was very kind and calmly said that he would help her get down. She was too high for him to reach, so he got a ladder. He talked to her softly and quietly and calmed her down. When he could reach her, he told her to put her arms around his neck and hang on. She hung on for dear life while he got them off the ladder and onto solid ground. At that point, she burst into tears and would not let go of Paul. He held her with a tenderness that was rare to see in a gangly sixteen-year-old boy. That day, they forged a bond. For years she liked Paul better than either of her brothers.

Her brothers had always treated her like she was a useless little girl. She was quite into dolls and fairy tale kingdoms until she was ten. Her father used to call her his little princess. She remembered the hundreds of times, from the time she was three or four to age eight, that her father came home, tired and exasperated, from work. The first thing that he always did was give his wife a long kiss. The boys would be clamoring for him to come and play catch or ball with them. Melissa would walk up to him, usually dressed in some fairy princess gown, look up at him with her curly dark hair and flushed pink cheeks, and quietly beg him to come to her tea party.

He would always reach down and hug and kiss her and tell her to get things ready and that he would be with her in ten minutes. He would get changed into comfortable clothes and tell the boys that he would play with them after supper. They always complained, but Roy would explain that he loved all of them and needed to spend time with each of them. Because Melly was younger, he would play with her in the afternoon. She went to bed shortly after supper. That would leave him plenty of time to play with the boys after supper.

Melissa even managed to get her dad to change into a prince's costume more than once. He laughingly told her that he only did

27

that when no one else was around. It would be their little secret. She giggled and was tickled pink to have such a fun secret with her daddy.

At age ten, her brothers tried to turn her into the younger brother they wanted. They practiced softball, basketball, volleyball, and hockey with her for several years until she was actually a pretty good player. Mark graduated from college by now, had his first disastrous love affair, and moved to New York. Melissa was twelve at that point. Matt rallied around and practiced sports with her for a few more years, but all too soon, he went away to college, as well.

Melissa grew up through her middle teen years without either of her brothers. She loved her parents dearly, but they were so devoted to each other that she sometimes felt a little left out. She didn't have that same kind of connection with her dad that she had when she was a little girl. Because she wanted her brothers to care about her, she outwardly gave up all her sweet fairytales. She had a more practical outlook on everything. That gained her brothers' approval but made her parents a little sad. Their little princess had moved on. She still came to them for advice and guidance, but she was more of a loner from age fourteen to eighteen. She still liked to spend time with her Grandma and Grandpa Hillman, though. They lived on a farm a few miles outside Litton.

Because of the heart attack that he endured when he was in his sixties, Grandpa Hillman did not work very much on the farm anymore. It was now being run by his other two sons. Melissa's uncles, Tom and John, each had a house on their father's farm. They were both married, and each had two sons. Melissa liked her cousins well enough but had little in common with them. She was the only granddaughter on both sides of the family, and all four of her grandparents treated her as if she was someone very special. It eased a little of her loneliness to hang out with them.

She remembered the hundreds of times that she walked, hand in hand, with Grandpa Hillman around the farm. Their favorite place to stop was the apple orchard. Grandpa Hillman taught her about apple growing and how to take care of the land. They always left the orchard with an apple in hand.

Grandma Hillman made the best apple butter in the world. Melissa asked her grandma to show her how to make that tasty treat when she was a teenager. Grandma Hillman enjoyed showing young Melissa how to cook and bake. Melissa was already a good cook by the time she was fifteen because she spent time cooking and baking with her mom and Grandma Harris, as well.

She liked to sit with her grandparents watching old movies on television. When she was a little girl, her Grandpa Hillman used to have her sit on his lap while they watched television. His strong arms held her close, and she always felt safe and loved.

* * *

A few years ago, Mark returned to Litton for Paul's wedding. Mark and Paul had been best friends for more than twenty years. Mark met Susan, fell in love with her, and decided to move back to Litton permanently. While Mark and Susan were engaged to be married, Susan was in a car accident and suffered from a Traumatic Brain Injury. She recuperated at Roy and Kay Hillman's house. Melissa had gotten to know and love Susan from that point on.

Melissa also had a lot of contact with Paul and his sweet wife, Sarah. After Christopher was born, Melissa often came to the rescue and babysat for him. Because she was single and did not have a steady boyfriend, she was readily available more often than their other friends. As a result, she and young Christopher were good buddies. She loved that little guy. His favorite toys right now were big colorful trucks. Since Melissa spent a lot of time at Paul and Sarah's home, she knew exactly which trucks Christopher had and which ones he would like.

Sarah dropped Christopher into Melissa's arms and rubbed her back. She was five months pregnant with their second child. "Melissa, you are a blessing to me. Thank you for taking Chris. He was wanting to see his Aunty Melly. Are you sure that you want to watch him tonight?" she asked anxiously.

"Sarah, I would love to sit with him tonight. I'll let him watch the guys play basketball, and when he gets tired of that, he and I will play with his new truck in the parking lot. Go sit down and relax, okay?" she said as she flashed Sarah a big smile.

Sarah hugged her and gratefully sat down on the camp chair that Paul always set up for her. Before the game started, Melissa watched Paul walk over to Sarah, caress her shiny hair, and gently touch her blossoming belly. He kissed her and then waved to Christopher before he went over to the youths to get the game started.

Melissa watched as Mark walked over to Susan and hugged and kissed her. Susan was eight months pregnant and so uncomfortable. She was a petite gal, and her huge belly made her look so out of proportion. Mark pressed a tender kiss onto her stomach and turned to go to the game. He waved at the women as he left them.

Melissa's brother, Matt, picked up his tiny wife, Tessa, and swung her around before giving her a big smacking kiss. He lovingly set her down and waved to the group of ladies before going to the game. Melissa thought that before long they would be announcing a pregnancy, as well.

Sometimes, just lately, she really felt on the outside of this group. They were all so in love with their spouses, having babies, and perfectly happy. She was the only one in the group who was single and had yet to meet the love of her life. With that thought, she looked down at Chris, who was wriggling around and waiting to be entertained.

She played with him and watched preparations for the weekly basketball game. As she observed her brothers getting the boys ready to play, she became aware of Erik Lundstrom. He was off to one side in the parking lot, showing a small ten-year-old boy how to dribble the basketball. Even though she was still mad at him, she had to admit that he was very kind and patient with the boy. Despite the difference in age and the remarkable difference in size, Erik's manner with the boy seemed to put him at ease.

While she was watching them, he looked up straight at her. They stared at each other for half a minute, neither of them with any expression on their face. He turned away, put his arm around the boy, and led him to the game.

Melissa played with Christopher and kept him busy during the game. She overheard Susan and Sarah talking about Erik Lundstrom. He had made a great impression on them. He volunteered at the project house every Saturday since they started building it. He was handy with power tools as well as that old-fashioned tool—the hammer. He stopped by the Shelter often to talk with Mark and help mentor the young boys. Apparently, he had broken up with his serious girlfriend, Diane, last year and had sworn off women ever since then.

Given this newfound information, Melissa now wondered if that was the reason for his unpleasant nature when they met. She felt a fleeting feeling of pity for him. But for some reason, she wanted to hold on to her feeling of dislike for him until he apologized to her for his unkind words. Deep in her heart, she knew that she was being pigheaded. She should just slough it off and get over it. Her feelings for him were complicated. She tried to hold on to her misgivings, even while she was starting to see that he was quite a decent guy.

Christopher started to act up, so she took him off to the side in the parking lot to play with his new truck. It was a large red and yellow one, and they had a grand time rolling it around. He was such a sweet boy that she could not help but smile and laugh with him. They missed the end of the game because they were into their play. It wasn't until she saw Paul start to walk over to them that she realized that the game was over. Paul picked up his son. After kissing the boy, he reached over and kissed Melissa's cheek.

"Melly, you lovely girl, thank you for taking Christopher off Sarah's hands tonight. She's been feeling a little under the weather with the new baby. It looks like Chris has a new truck. Melly, you spoil him," he told her with a friendly grin for her.

Melissa looked up at Paul and grinned. "He's my boyfriend. Of course, I would bring him gifts. He is the sweetest and cutest young man that I know," she said saucily.

Paul grinned and told her that she should come over to their house tonight and relax. They were having a few people over to have some snacks and cool drinks. Melissa agreed to follow them home.

Erik watched Melissa laughing and playing with Paul's little boy. *She's such a natural with kids,* he thought. He had a hard time concentrating on the game. His gaze kept going toward the parking lot where Melissa was playing with Chris. He wished that he could stop thinking about her. As he dwelt upon their mutual gaze earlier tonight, he gathered that she had not forgiven him and still disliked him. He really wished that he could talk with her. The longer this impasse continued without his apology, the harder it became to apologize. He told Paul that he couldn't stop off at his house. Erik did not want another evening in which Melissa kept herself as far away from him as she could.

CHAPTER

FOUR

Erik had Melissa's next order in his hand. She had emailed it to his company just like she said she would. He printed it off and walked into Tollie's Grocery Store. He waved to the regular workers and walked back to the staff lounge.

He intently looked around and eventually saw Melissa. She was dealing with an older couple and smiling at them. Her curly dark hair was pulled into a loose ponytail, but some curls had escaped and framed her face beguilingly. He felt a strong urge to go forward and tuck her curly hair behind her ears. She was wearing long shiny gold earrings, and they kept swinging back and forth whenever she moved. He thought that she looked very pretty when she smiled.

He wondered if she would ever smile at him. Every single time that he had seen her, she was smiling or laughing with someone. Then, inevitably, when she caught sight of him, the smile would abruptly leave her face, and she would blankly look at him and move away.

This was getting ridiculous. He was furious with himself for wanting to catch a glimpse of her as often as he could. He could not stop thinking about her, and he hated that. He certainly did not need any entanglements in his life right now. He had his work to think about. It was just fine that she hated him. That made it easier for him to keep his distance—although he did like to see her when she smiled. That smile brightened her whole face, and the sun practically shone out of her eyes.

Melissa looked up and saw Erik. He always looked like a big bad Viking to her. She thought that this was not a suitable job for him. He should be out in the forest cutting down trees or pillaging and plundering some village. She shook her head at her fanciful thoughts. She did not want to talk with him. She walked to the back of the store, spoke to a cashier who was walking past her, and entered her office. She closed the door sharply and locked it.

The cashier came over to Erik, smiled, and said, "Hello, Mr. Lundstrom. Ms. Hillman asked me to take any forms that you might have for her. She asked to be excused, but she had some urgent business to attend to." The cashier looked at Erik and waited for him to speak or give her something.

Erik just shook his head no and said curtly, "No, thanks anyway. I will just send it to her in an email. Thank you for your message. Goodbye." With that, he turned on his heel and left the store. Obviously, Melissa was still not speaking to him. Fine, two could play at that game. He didn't have to talk with her, either. His conscience still told him that he was the one who needed to make the apology, not her. *Well, I will when I am good and ready,* he thought darkly.

He thought about it for another week and finally arrived at the conclusion that Melissa had no intention of allowing him to get near enough to her to verbally apologize. He would have to apologize in some other way. He decided to send Melissa some flowers and a note with the apology written on it. It was the only way that he would be able to live with himself. He felt guilty for upsetting her. He could tell that she was a very nice woman.

Erik wondered if they would ever get past this, even if she accepted his apology. He truly hoped so. He saw her quite frequently at the project house or at one of her brother's homes. He was fed up with the fact that she consistently ignored him. He wanted to talk with her and see her smile at him, just once. Then, maybe he could forget about her and move on. As it was now, he thought about her way too much. It was infuriating.

Melissa was surprised when a large bunch of summer flowers in a cellophane wrapper arrived for her at work one afternoon. One of the cashiers brought them in as she sat in her newly decorated tiny office. It was only big enough for her desk and a few small chairs. Because the day was a warm one, Melissa's office door was open. She felt like she was in a closet when she closed the door. It also got as hot as blazes in there when the door was shut. The cashier peaked her head around the open door and asked Melissa, "Ms. Hillman, are you free for a minute?"

"Yes, come on in," replied Melissa. The cashier came in and set the flowers on Melissa's desk with a flourish.

"Here you go, Ms. Hillman. They just arrived by Special Delivery. There's a card in there, the man said. Must be from your boyfriend," she said cheekily to Melissa.

Melissa thanked her and told her that she should go back to her counter. She opened the flowers first. They were a lovely large bunch of beautiful fragrant summer flowers. She bent her head and took a big whiff of them. She wondered if they were from the Olson brothers in appreciation for all her hard work.

She smiled as she opened the card. As she read it, her eyes opened wide, and she couldn't believe what she was reading. The card said, "To Melissa Hillman. I want to formally apologize for my unkind words to you the first day we met. I was wrong, and I am sorry, more than I can say. Please forgive me." It was signed by Erik Lundstrom.

Melissa couldn't believe what she just read. Then and there, she decided to accept his apology. They would probably never be friends, but at least this apology would clear the air. She put the flowers in a vase that she found in the back storeroom and set them on the corner of her desk. They made the whole tiny room smell glorious. She put the notecard in her purse and sat down at her computer.

After a quick moment of thinking, she pulled up Erik's email address at his company's website and typed in, "To Erik Lundstrom. Thank you for the beautiful flowers and the apology. I will accept your apology. Sincerely, Melissa Hillman."

She took the flowers home with her that evening. They sat on her kitchen table for a week until they wilted. Resisting the impulse to throw them out, she instead decided to make a dried flower arrangement out of them. Musing to herself, she thought, *since I waited this long to get an apology, I may as well have a keepsake.*

Erik looked at Melissa's email to him and grinned widely. He immediately thought, *she has accepted my apology! Now if we could only get on better terms with each other.* He would look for his chance, he promised himself.

The next Saturday at the construction site, Melissa and Brad were again partners as they painted a wall. She saw Erik arrive. She smiled shyly at him and waved to him. He waved back at her. Because Melissa was with Brad, Erik did not feel like going over to talk to her. He hoped that they would have the chance to talk and clear the air. He was so happy that she accepted his apology. However, he was not about to say anything of a personal nature to Melissa when she was with Brad.

They spent the day at the construction site without ever saying a word to each other. Melissa had been hoping that Erik would come over to talk with her. She was disappointed when it seemed as if he was avoiding her. Maybe he only apologized to her because of their business connection. Maybe he personally did not want to get to know her. She felt a little sad about that. She thought about him quite a lot since his apology. She knew that he had sworn off women, but she hoped that they could at least be cordial to each other.

*   *   *

Melissa enjoyed the summer with her family. She had been working at Tollie's for several months. She volunteered at the project house whenever she had a free Saturday. They were set to finish the first house by Friday evening. On Saturday, there would be a big picnic at the park a few miles from the Shelter. There was talk of frisbee golf, volleyball, a softball game, and even swimming. Melissa was happy that the picnic fell on her free Saturday.

Since Mark had gotten his parents to volunteer at the construction site a few Saturdays, they were also invited. That Saturday, Melissa stopped first at her parents' house. They were planning to attend the picnic. Susan was almost a week overdue to have her baby. Kay Hillman wanted to sit with Susan and remind her as often as necessary to just relax and let others take care of things. Susan was such a go-getter that Mark had a tough time getting her to take things easy. Melissa drove her car to the park with her parents on board. Mom sat in the back with all the food that they were bringing.

She parked her car, and they all carried the food to the pavilion. Melissa had made a triple batch of her famous caramel nut brownies, and she was anxious to display them, looking inviting and delicious, on a pretty tray. She helped her sisters-in-law put out all the food. The plan was to have a game of frisbee golf and then eat lunch. After lunch, they would have their softball game. Those who didn't want to play softball could play volleyball or go swimming.

Melissa was happy to see that her brownies were going fast, even before lunchtime. It made her feel good that everyone seemed to like them so much and couldn't help but smile inwardly as she thought about the early takers "ruining their lunch" by eating dessert first. She saw Erik the minute he got there. He brought a bunch of ice and different varieties of soft drinks. He came into the pavilion to set up the cold drinks station while Melissa helped to put out the food. He nodded to her and smiled briefly but said nothing. She nodded back, unsmiling.

She watched as he snuck a brownie on his way back out. He had it in his mouth, chewing it. Then he stopped walking, came back, and took two more. *Well, here is someone who really likes my brownies*, Melissa thought with an impish grin.

The frisbee golf game was very fun. Melissa had a wonderful time playing it. Her team won the game. She whooped it up as much as the rest of her team. They all went back to the pavilion for lunch. Melissa noticed that Susan was sweating and very quiet. This was unusual for Susan since she was an outgoing young woman. Melissa took her plate of food over to sit next to Susan.

Mark had been hanging around Susan all morning, and Susan kept sending him away saying that she was fine. Mark watched her like a hawk from wherever he was standing. This was their first baby, and he was anxious for Susan. He loved her so much. Ever since Mark had almost lost Susan in a car accident, he tended to be quite attentive to her every need.

Melissa talked with Susan in the calmest way she could. She wondered if Susan started her labor. Susan was pale. As Melissa sat there, she noticed Susan make a grimace and catch her breath. Susan didn't say anything and pretended that nothing happened. Melissa stood up and asked Susan if she needed anything to drink or eat. Susan just shook her head no, but she seemed to grit her teeth.

Melissa walked over to where Mark was standing and drew him aside. She discreetly told Mark what she had seen. It looked to her as if Susan was in labor. Mark looked shocked for a second. He quickly walked over to Susan and sat next to her. He gently laid her head onto his chest and stroked her sweaty head. Taking her hand in his, he quietly talked with her. He asked her if she was starting labor. She gave a nod, and he gently pulled her to her feet and led her to their car, his arm around her shoulder.

He glanced at Melissa and nodded to her. She nodded back and went to find her mom and dad. When she found them, she told them that Mark was taking Susan to the hospital since Susan was going into labor. Her mom and dad wanted to go with them to the hospital, but they didn't have their car. Melissa told them to take hers and gave her dad the keys. She said that she would find someone at the picnic who would drop her off at her apartment. Kay and Roy left right away to go to the hospital to support Mark. Kay was so excited that her first grandchild was about to be born.

Melissa went to tell Matt, Tessa, Paul, and Sarah what was happening. Sarah was Susan's very best friend, and she and Paul wanted to go to the hospital to be with Mark, too. Matt and Tessa promised to watch little Christopher and then take him home with them. They, along with Melissa, often babysat for Christopher when Sarah and Paul needed to go somewhere. News of Susan's labor spread quickly, and people stood around gossiping and talking about it.

No one was watching the little six-year-old boy when he grew disinterested with all the adult conversation and decided to go into the pool by himself. Of course, he did not bother to tell anyone else of his plan. When his mother noticed that he was missing, she became alarmed, so everyone spread out and started looking for him.

Melissa remembered that he had been whining earlier about wanting to go into the pool, so she headed there first. She got there within two minutes and frantically looked around. She did not see him. She walked around the sides of the pool and finally saw his small arm come out of the water for a brief second.

She was a strong swimmer and didn't hesitate before diving into the pool. She dragged him out of the pool and flipped him over. He was not breathing. She immediately started to try to resuscitate him. She was still working on him when Erik and Matt got there. Melissa was getting tired, and Erik quickly and wordlessly took over for her.

The little boy coughed up a lungful of water and started to bawl. Melissa and Erik just knelt on the concrete trying to catch their breath. The boy's mom ran over, dropped to her knees, and gathered her son in her arms. She was crying and rocking back and forth with him in her arms.

She looked at Erik and said in an extremely shaky voice, "Thank you so much! You saved my boy. I can never repay you. God Bless you." She went over to him and tried to hug him even with her boy still in her arms. Erik looked at her and then at Melissa.

His voice was quiet but clear. "Melissa is the person whom you should thank. She is the one who dragged him out of the water and started CPR on him. I came along after the fact and just finished what she started." He looked at Melissa and smiled nicely at her. For the first time, she smiled happily back at him. He felt that smile all the way down to his toes.

The boy's mother came over to hug and kiss Melissa. There were quite a few people around by this time, and there was a lot of talk about Melissa's quick thinking and actions. Melissa tried to shrug it off with a flush on her face. She was heralded as a heroine. She just kept shaking her head and saying that it could have been anyone.

Matt flung his arm around Melissa and walked her back to the pavilion. The boy and his parents drove off to take him to the clinic to get checked out. The excitement of the day was too much, and people decided to call it a day and go home.

Melissa, Tessa, and several of the other ladies started to clear up all the food. The men gathered up all the athletic equipment. Melissa looked around and wondered who she would ask to give her a ride home. Tessa and Matt had little Christopher and all his stuff, along with their food and supplies, so they didn't really have room in their car.

Erik heard Melissa talking to Tessa and quietly said, "I'll take you home, Melissa. I have lots of room in my car for the food and leftover stuff. I know that you need to bring back Mark and Susan's stuff, as well." He looked at Melissa with bright inquiring eyes.

She swallowed hard and nodded, saying, "Thank you, Erik. I appreciate that. Are you sure you can get all of this stuff in your car?"

"No problem. Have you seen my car? It's big enough to take all that and more," he grinned as he responded.

"Okay, lead the way. I'll follow you," Melissa told Erik.

After Melissa said goodbye to Matt and Tessa, Erik set off to his car. He was carrying a huge load of supplies. Melissa followed him carrying her own load of leftover food. Erik stopped next to a shiny blue Ford Escape. He opened the back and started to pile the stuff inside. Melissa stood next to him and handed over her leftovers and watched him fit them all in, sort of like a jigsaw puzzle. They had to go back to the pavilion for another load. When they had loaded everything, they said a quiet good night to the few people who were still there.

Back in the car, Erik turned to Melissa and said, "You'll have to direct me. I have no idea where you live."

Melissa gave him directions to her apartment. They decided to leave Mark and Susan's sporting equipment in his car. Erik would drop it off at Mark's house another time. There was no need to lug it all inside Melissa's apartment only to lug it back out again in a day or so. He helped her carry the leftover food up to her apartment. She would store it in her fridge and share it with her family tomorrow.

Clarabelle, the cat, met them at the door. She looked up at Melissa and immediately started to meow. She obviously wanted her supper. Melissa put her load of food into the fridge and picked up the cat. "Hey, Puss, I will get your supper in a minute. Hang on, okay?" she asked the cat.

Erik grinned at her and said, "I wouldn't have pegged you as a cat woman. You seem more like a dog person to me."

"It's funny you say that. You're exactly right. I do love dogs. We always had dogs when I was growing up, but they are all gone now. Clarabelle, here, is a refugee who currently lives in comfort with me. My next-door neighbor, Mrs. Simpkins, had to go into a care facility. Her daughter and son-in-law came to move her possessions out. There was nowhere for the cat to go. They were going to either send Clarabelle to the pound or have her put down. I've known Clarabelle for several years, and I couldn't let that happen to her, so I invited her to live with me. It's not the best arrangement, but at least she is free and alive. I don't have a ton of free time to spend with her, but she is somewhat self-sufficient. She doesn't seem to mind being alone for most of the day."

Erik personally thought that it was a very nice thing for Melissa to have done. He said, "I have an Irish setter named Rusty. He's an awesome fellow and a darn good friend to me. I've never been around a cat. Do you think that she will let me pick her up and pet her?"

"Give it a try. I can't guarantee that she won't try to scratch you, though. She doesn't seem to like everyone. I had to hold on to her when they were moving Mrs. Simpkins out. She certainly did not like her daughter's husband. He had a couple of long scratches to show for it," Melissa remembered with a chuckle.

Erik cautiously picked up Clarabelle and cuddled her in his big arms. Clarabelle's loud raucous purring was proof that she liked him. Erik looked down at her and grinned. He said with a surprised voice, "Well, what do you know? I guess she likes me."

"I guess so," said Melissa. She briefly wondered how it would feel to be held in strong arms such as those.

Erik stood there holding the cat and looking around at Melissa's comfortable and attractive apartment. He thought about his bare house. He had no wall hangings, rugs, or decorations of any kind. It was basically four bare walls and only a modicum of basic functional furniture. Here was an example of someone who really knew how to make a beautiful home for herself.

Melissa looked down at her still wet clothes and grimaced. She wanted to get out of these clothes as soon as possible, but she wanted to talk with Erik for just a minute, too. She wondered if he would stay while she changed.

She caught his eye and quietly said, "Thank you for the ride home, Erik. Would you mind waiting here for just a few minutes while I get into some dry clothes? I'd like the chance to talk with you for a few seconds." She looked steadily at him.

Erik nodded and said, "Yes, go ahead and change. It will give me the chance to look around your lovely apartment. You really have a lot of things in here. My house is bare in comparison." He smiled kindly at her.

Melissa said, "Thank you. I'll only take a minute," and went into her bedroom. She came back quickly dressed in a pretty pink sundress and her pink slippers.

Erik was perusing her living room, considering what each item might say about Melissa. Hearing her enter the room, he turned around and grinned at Melissa. Her breath caught in her throat as she saw that. He really had a very nice face when he grinned like that.

She sat in her most comfortable armchair. It was floral printed, and Melissa, in her pink dress, was the perfect complement to the room. Erik scanned the room in search of something a bit bigger for him. He was a big man and needed a man-sized chair. He decided to try out the hunter green leather sofa. He held on to Clarabelle as he perched at the edge of the sofa and looked at Melissa. He waited calmly for her to speak.

Melissa knew that she needed to say something first. After all, Erik had broken the ice with his flowers and a note of apology. She looked at him squarely in the eyes, and said in her quiet voice, "I just wanted to thank you in person for your nice apology and the beautiful flowers. I am so glad that you did that. I was being pigheaded about not speaking to you. We are two professionals who should have been better at communicating. So, thank you, and I'm sorry, too." She held out her hand as if to say, let's shake on it.

Erik felt a rush of tenderness for her come over him at her apology. He took her hand for a moment before he let it go. He smiled gently at Melissa and stroked Clarabelle's soft fur. "Thank you, Melissa, for that. I am glad that we got over that mess. Do you think that we could be friends or at least colleagues who can talk normally with each other? We seem to run into each other quite a bit. It's so much easier if we are speaking to each other, don't you think?" He asked her in a serious, yet friendly, voice.

Melissa's gaze was drawn to the sight of his big hands stroking her cat so gently. For a moment, she recalled his gentleness with the boy at the basketball game. She raised her eyes to his face and answered with a small smile, "Yes, we can at least talk with each other. It may take a little while to become friendly. We have had such a weird start, but I am willing to try if you are."

"Good, thank you, Melissa. Now that we're speaking to each other again, I hope that you'll call me Erik, instead of Mr. Lundstrom. Before I go, will you tell me a little about this room? Did you decorate it yourself, and if so, how did you know how to do it? I wasn't kidding you; I have nothing on my walls or floor and absolutely no knick-knacks. While I would never furnish my place as much as you have, I know that I need to do something. It really is worse than a sterile hotel room," he said as he shook his head exasperatingly.

Melissa must have been either pleased or amused at his explanation, for she smiled genuinely at him. Erik felt his heart clench when he saw her beautiful smile for him. Oh, no, he was in for it. He was starting to have feelings for this sweet young woman. Diane and her poison were starting to fade, and right now he was only seeing and thinking about Melissa.

Melissa told him, "Well, I just buy what I like. No one showed me what to buy or how to decorate. I like antiques, wood, and wrought iron. I hunt in antique stores and at flea markets to find what I'm looking for. On occasion, something that I think will go great with something else ends up being a flop. At other times the most incongruent things work well together. I guess it's just trial and error."

"What do you do with the things that don't work together?" he asked her with growing interest.

"Well, if I've spent a lot of money on it, I try to fit it in somewhere else. Otherwise, I give it away to my family or friends or even Goodwill," she told him.

"Okay, thank you, Melissa. That gives me something to think about. I'll try to remember that when I am looking for something for my house," he said to her. He wished that they were friends and that he could ask her to help him decorate his house with him.

Melissa wished that they were friends so that she could offer to help him decorate his house. She was curious about it and wished that he would invite her over to see it. She just loved to decorate houses and apartments. She and Sarah had often talked about their mutual interest in interior decorating.

"Well, I should get going. Thanks for your decorating advice, Melissa," Erik said as he stood up from the couch. He handed Clarabelle to her. She carefully set the cat down on the floor.

"Thank you, again, for the ride home. I really appreciated it," Melissa said as she walked Erik to the door. She remembered the leftover food in the fridge.

"Erik, would you like any of the leftover food for your supper?" she asked him. "There is absolutely tons of it left."

"Well, if you have any of those wonderful brownies left, I would take some of those. Do you know who brought them? I'd like to ask that person where they got them," he asked with a good-natured smile.

Melissa grinned, went to the cupboard, and took out the ones that she had kept back from the picnic. She handed him the container and said, "Well, you can ask me then. I brought them."

"Really? Where did you buy them? That bakery must make a fortune on them!" Erik said excitedly.

Melissa just smiled bigger and said, "I made them. They are my secret famous caramel nut brownies. I am well known for them in my family circle."

"You did?!" Erik exclaimed in disbelief. "Those are absolutely the best brownies that I have ever tasted in my whole life. And that's saying a lot because I have eaten a lot of brownies in my life. It is my absolute favorite dessert."

Melissa decided to tease him just a little and said, "Well, buster, don't think that you are going to con me out of my secret famous recipe because you can't. I'll go to my grave with that little secret."

Erik smiled and nodded, "Understood. Well, I hope that I will get invited to another picnic sometime to which you will bring your secret famous caramel nut brownies. I might just sneak the whole plateful down my shirt. Not that I need them—I'm too big as it is," he said ruefully as he looked down at his big chest.

"No, don't think like that, Erik," Melissa discounted his words with a gentle smile, "You're just a really big guy. It takes more to feed you than other people. But your big muscles come in handy when you're helping to build a house and when there is a heavy load to be carried. It takes all kinds to make the world, as my Grandma always said."

"Well, thanks. I'll try not to eat all of these on my way home," he said with a grateful sigh.

"Where do you live, the next state over?" she teased him gently.

He just shook his head and daringly bent to lightly kiss her cheek. "Thanks, again for the marvelous brownies. I'll get this container back to you the next time I volunteer at the Shelter, okay?" he smiled at her as he opened the door.

Melissa nodded and said, "That's fine. I'm sure that I'll see you sometime soon. Enjoy those brownies and try to save at least two of them for your lunch tomorrow. Bye."

She smiled as the door shut behind him. She thought about the kiss on her cheek. It was a sweet thing to do. She was glad that he had not tried to kiss her on the lips. It was too soon. They had barely begun speaking to each other. On the other hand, she had enjoyed gently teasing him. He was a much nicer person than she had ever thought possible. She hoped that they could become friends in time.

Erik left Melissa's apartment with her brownies. As he sat in his car for a few minutes he thought about Melissa. He had really enjoyed talking with her and teasing her a little this evening. He no longer thought about Diane and the issues they had. He found himself totally enchanted by Melissa. He had dared to kiss her cheek. That felt so nice. He wondered if he would ever get the chance to properly kiss those lovely lips. Probably not. He had totally forgotten about her boyfriend, Brad. At the construction site, he had heard someone call that guy Brad, so he knew her boyfriend's name. It was just his luck—he finally met a woman that he liked, and she was already taken.

CHAPTER
FIVE

Because Melissa's parents still had her car, she couldn't go to the hospital to see Mark and hear how Susan was. She called Mark on his cell phone.

"Mark, what's happening? Is Susan doing okay?" Melissa asked her brother.

"Oh, hi, Melly. The doctor said that it will probably be a while. Susan is not dilated very much yet. They said it might take until sometime tomorrow for her to have the baby. I have been sitting with her, but she was tired and wanted to try to take a nap, so now I'm out here in the waiting room with everyone. I'll probably send Mom and Dad home in a little while. I'll send them to your apartment to pick you up. That way you will have your car back. Then you can take them to their house. Sarah and Paul will stay for another hour or two to keep me company. They just called Matt. He and Tessa are going to keep Christopher with them until tomorrow. That way Sarah can come back when Susan gets closer to having the baby."

"Oh, good. Thanks for telling me. Do you need anything, Mark?" asked Melissa.

"What happened to all of our equipment and stuff?" asked Mark.

"It's in Erik's car. He dropped me off at my apartment with all the leftover food. He decided to keep your stuff in his car and will drop it off at your house in a day or two when you are home," she told him.

"Erik took you home?" Mark was incredulous. He continued, "I thought that you hated him, Melly. Have you changed your mind about him?" Then he couldn't resist quickly adding, "Susan and I really like him."

"Yeah, we worked through that initial issue. We're not friends, but at least we are talking to each other," she told him.

"I'm glad, Melly. It would have been difficult to ignore each other when you seem to be at the same place as each other quite often." Then, changing the topic, Mark inquired, "Say, what's this I hear from Matt that you are the little heroine of the day?"

"Oh, I just got there first. Anyone would have done what I did," Melissa modestly responded.

"Just the same, we are all so proud of you, Melly. You saved that little boy's life. Nice work, little sis," Mark said with admiration.

"Thanks," Melissa told him. "Let me talk with Mom for a second, okay?" Mark agreed and handed his phone to his mother.

Melissa and her mom made some plans for the rest of the evening. She hung up and went into the kitchen to hunt through the leftovers in the fridge. She planned to give most of the food to her parents. People would probably be stopping by their house tomorrow to find out about Mark and Susan and the baby.

Later that evening, Melissa's parents came over to pick her up. She drove them back to their house with a big load of leftovers. Once there, they put away the food, and then they talked for a while. They all promised to keep in touch about the baby. Melissa finally took herself home after a very late supper. She was tired. It had been a long and exciting day.

The next morning, she called Mark at the hospital. He answered briefly but told her to hang up and call Sarah, instead. Melissa called Sarah and learned that Susan's labor had progressed, and she would probably have the baby within the hour. Melissa hung up and drove straight to the hospital to be there when the baby arrived.

She arrived to find the waiting room full of people. In addition to Sarah and Paul, Susan's parents and Melissa's parents were there. Matt and Tessa were also there with Christopher.

Mark and Susan had not told anyone about the sex of the baby. They wanted to keep it a secret until the baby arrived. They already had names picked out. The baby was going to be named either Sarah Rose Hillman or Paul Matthew Hillman.

At 10:55 am, Mark came triumphantly out of Susan's room and addressed the people in the waiting room, "Well, Sarah Rose Hillman is finally here. Susan and the baby are doing very well."

His face was flushed, and tears were falling down his cheeks. He had the biggest, happiest, tenderest smile that Melissa had ever seen on him. Everyone laughed and hugged, talking a mile a minute. After a few minutes, Mark excused himself to go back to Susan. The rest of the family talked and made plans for a happy get-together.

Melissa's parents invited everyone to an impromptu party that afternoon at their home. Melissa promised to drive her car behind theirs and help her mom with the food for the party. Since Mark and Susan had waited for the baby's arrival before they had their baby shower, the family would start to plan the shower that afternoon. Mark promised to call them that afternoon and check-in.

Melissa couldn't wait to start to buy cute little baby girl clothes for her very first niece. This was Kay and Roy's first grandchild. *Boy, was Sarah Rose going to be a cherished and pampered little princess,* thought Melissa with a happy smile.

The shower planned and the date set, Melissa thought that she would go to the flea market the next Saturday that she was free and see if she could find anything special for baby Sarah's room. She wanted to buy an antique doll carriage if she could find one. Additionally, Melissa was hoping to find a red cardinal figurine for Susan's upcoming birthday.

She asked Brad to go with her, but he had other plans for the day. Melissa set off with her huge folded bag and hoped for success. It was a hot and sunny day, so she pulled her hair up into a bun and wore her coolest shorts and a sleeveless top.

The biggest flea market was on the edge of town and located in a twenty-acre field. She had been there several times in the past and knew just where to start looking for the doll carriage if there was one to be had.

She had a cold bottle of water in a holder around her neck. Hunting for treasures was hot and thirsty work. There were food vendors within the flea market in case it took longer than she planned, and she got hungry.

With a happy heart, Melissa entered the market and headed to her favorite stalls. She spent about an hour looking around at everything before she found just what she was looking for. It was an antique baby carriage constructed of white wicker and had a ruffled lacy white cover. It was quite a lot more money than she planned to spend, but it was exactly what she wanted to give her baby niece.

She handed over the money for the carriage and was just wondering how to carry it back to her car when she saw Erik walking in her direction. Melissa had opened her large bag, but the carriage was too big to fit in it. Erik saw Melissa and walked up to her. He looked so different in a t-shirt and cargo shorts. They seemed to fit his big muscular body so much better than the suit that he wore on his job.

"Well, hello there. I never thought that I would see you here, Erik," said Melissa.

He studied the doll carriage and said, "Hi. I bet that thing is for Mark and Susan's baby, isn't it?"

"Yes, I wanted to get baby Sarah her first doll carriage. It's perfect. Now I just need to get it to my car. It's too big to fit in my bag, and I don't know if I can carry it all the way back to my car. I could put it down and roll it all of the way there, but I don't want to wear out the wheels on this dusty and rough ground." Melissa frowned as she contemplated her choices.

"Well, I would be willing to carry it to your car…for a price," he told her with a big grin.

"What is your price? I have already spent far too much money on this thing," she retorted.

"I will carry it for you if you agree to help me look around for some things to decorate my home. I seem to be hopeless at it. I've been here for a couple of hours already, and I don't have a clue about what I want to buy. What do you think? Do we have a deal?" he asked in a pleading voice.

Melissa was happy to agree. She wanted the carriage to stay in good condition. "Yes, I agree to your terms," she said happily.

"Okay, lead the way to your car. Let's get this taken care of before we look around for my stuff. I promise not to keep you all day, though. If you can even give me a hint about what I should buy, I will be very grateful," he told her.

Melissa watched him gently cradle the carriage in his strong arms. She fleetingly wondered what it would feel like to be held close in those enormous arms. *Silly,* she rebuked herself. *You don't have that kind of relationship with him.*

She led the way to her car. He carefully put it in her trunk on top of the old blanket that she kept in there for that very purpose. He dusted his hands off and swiped a hand across his sweaty brow.

"Boy, it's hot out here. You were smart to bring some bottled water with you," he said.

"I'd offer you some, but I'm afraid that it's all gone," she said with regret.

"I saw some food vendors inside the gate. Let me buy you a cold drink and maybe some food. Have you had lunch? Are you hungry?" he asked her as they walked.

"No, I haven't had lunch yet. I could go for something. But you don't have to buy me anything. I have money," she told him quickly.

"I think my part of the deal was easier than yours will be. I would like to buy you lunch for helping me. Is that okay?" he asked her.

"Alright, if you say so," she agreed.

They found the food vendors and decided on sub sandwiches, watermelon, and cold lemonade. There were a few picnic tables next to the food vendors. They sat down and ate their lunch. While they ate, Melissa asked him about the colors of his walls and carpet.

He told her that everything was a dreary beige or tan color. He had a brown couch and matching chairs, along with an entertainment system in his living room. That was about all there was in there. Melissa's eyes got wide. She couldn't even imagine living in such a sparsely furnished room.

"What kind of things do you like? I mean, do you like a sports theme? Or maybe nautical or western? If you don't have any preference about the theme, do you have some favorite colors that you might like in your living room?" she asked him.

"Hmm, I don't really know. I do like blues and greens, and maybe some red colors. I think that I might know what I like when I see it. Right now, nothing is coming to mind. Do you see that I need help? I'm hopeless at this," he complained in a light voice. He hoped that Melissa would still want to help him. He knew that he was not being very helpful to her.

Melissa loved a challenge. She wanted to find some things that Erik would love to have in his home. "Let's start with one room in mind, first. Which room do you want us to focus on?" she asked him.

"Definitely the living room. I spend the most amount of time there when I am at home," he told her.

"Okay, let's start there. Do you have any plans to paint there or change your carpet or furniture?" she asked.

Erik frowned and said, "No, I had not planned to do any of those things. I thought that I could just add to the little that was already there."

"Sure, we can add color to the room by the pieces we buy for it. You said you liked blues and greens. Do you like the ocean or beach?" she asked him.

"Yes, I do like water a lot. I love mountains and forests and big deep blue lakes. Think about Colorado or somewhere like that," he told her, starting to get interested in their project.

"Great, I have a few ideas. Let's go and find you a new living room," she said with enthusiasm.

She jumped up and reached over to pull him to his feet. He held her hand for a second or so before letting it go.

He smiled at her and said, "Okay, teacher, lead the way. I am your student for the day."

Melissa took him to some of her favorite stalls. They ended up finding a few great scenic pictures of the Rocky Mountains. When she found a lovely wild stallion figure, she held it up and said, "This might go great on an end table. It would fit with the pictures and your color scheme. Do you like it?"

Erik nodded and said enthusiastically, "I love horses. I used to ride all the time when I still lived at home. Let's buy it. It will look great in my living room. Now, what else?"

Melissa was glad that she had kept her large bag with her. The vendor wrapped up the horse figure carefully, and they put it in the bag. Erik took the bag from her and slung it over his shoulder and said, "Let me take this. It's going to get too heavy for you. I'm stronger than you are. Let me do all of the carrying from now on, okay?"

Melissa said, "Well, I can't compete with your muscles, that's for sure." She smiled at him. Erik felt very content and wanted to continue their easy communication.

"How much longer do you have? I don't want to make you trudge around here all day. Please let me know if you need to go. But let's go through these last few stalls, first, okay? I would love to find a few more things like that stallion. Or maybe some throw pillows or something that will add a bit more color to the room. Is that okay with you?" he asked her.

"I'm okay for a bit, yet. I have time. Let's look in this next stall. I have found great things here in the past," she said.

"Thanks," he told her as they walked to the next stall.

When Melissa found a small rustic canoe made of birch, she took it to Erik for him to see. They decided that it would go well with the pictures of the Rocky Mountains. It would be wonderful if they could find some deer or other woodland animals to put on an end table with the canoe.

They saw so many things that Melissa would have loved to buy for her own apartment, but she really didn't need anything new. Erik gently teased her that she was supposed to be finding things for his home, not hers.

He watched Melissa's face when she laughed at him. Her smile and laughter warmed his heart. He wished that they could always be this open and comfortable with each other. He also wished that Melissa wasn't dating Brad; he would like to ask her out on a date. The more time they spent together, the more he saw that they had quite a lot of things in common. He was just grateful for the time they had together today, though.

Melissa was enjoying her search for the perfect knick-knacks for Erik's house. Even though she had never been in his house, she was starting to get a good idea of how it would look, given the right decorations. She pictured the living room in her mind—full of outdoor woodsy or mountainous scenes and majestic animals.

She wanted to find the perfect decorations for his home. *Deep blues, greens, and browns are a nice combination for a man's house,* she thought.

Melissa found a painted wooden carving of two deer in a green wooded setting and held it up for Erik to see. He exclaimed, "I love that!" Happy with his enthusiasm, Melissa redoubled her efforts to find the perfect decorations for his living room.

They continued to look around and found a deep blue and green cotton rug for the space in front of the couch and some throw pillows that matched the colors in the rug. They bought them and added them to the bag, which was bulging by now.

They decided that they would look in one more stall before they took everything to Erik's car. Besides the baby carriage for Sarah Rose, Melissa wanted to buy a birthday gift for Susan, whose birthday was in a few weeks. Susan loved birds.

Melissa found a lovely red cardinal. Susan had recently mentioned to Melissa that they were her favorite Minnesota bird, but she did not have any in her collection. She never bought any birds for herself because she knew that others liked to give them to her for her birthday, Christmas, or as a souvenir from their trips.

The cardinal was intricately carved with a wealth of detail on its tiny head and wings. It stood on a small branch with wings spread wide as if it was ready to soar away. Melissa grabbed it and held on to it while she looked around some more.

She saw a dear little pair of black-capped chickadees residing together on a thin branch. The chubby little birds were adorable. Their painted colors were bright, as were their bright black eyes. It was strange because they looked so loving toward each other—if birds could be that. The male had his head cocked to the side and somehow had a tender look on his tiny face as he looked at his mate. Melissa could swear that the female was smiling behind her beak.

The overall aura was one of tenderness and care. Melissa was enchanted with it. She liked birds, but she didn't know where she would put them in her apartment. She carried it around with her while they looked for more items for Erik. She was going to buy the cardinal for Susan's birthday gift but held on to the chickadees while she debated whether to buy them for herself.

In that same stall, she found a sweet little red fox and fat beaver. They would be cute on one of Erik's end tables. When she asked him about them, he grinned and said that if she thought they would go well with the other things they bought, he would buy them, as well. He liked woodland creatures.

He hunted through the stall looking at everything. He gave a small shout of joy when he found a rustic picture frame. There were resin people and a small rowboat attached to the frame. Blond figures of a young boy and man were fly fishing. The man had his arm around the boy.

Erik's face was flushed with deep emotion. He turned to Melissa and said softly, "This could be my dad and me. He used to take me fly fishing when I was a boy. Some of my favorite memories are of camping and fishing with him. He was a blond man, just like I am. I have a favorite picture of him that I'm going to put in this frame. It will go well on the wall with the pictures of the mountains, don't you think?"

Melissa nodded. She thought that Erik might have lost his dad. She carefully asked, "Erik, I'm sorry to ask you this, but did you lose your dad?"

Erik looked sad for a moment before he said, "Yes, my dad died suddenly of a heart attack when I was sixteen. Mom and I didn't even know that he had a heart defect until his death. It's been almost twenty years, and we still miss him. He was a wonderful man, and I adored him. I try to pattern my life after his. I know that might be hard for you to believe, after the shaky beginning that we had, but I really do want to emulate his life. I'd like to think that I will love my own children the way he loved and cared for me."

Melissa was touched by his words and obvious love for his father. She had heard her brothers say something similar when they talked about their own father, even though he was still very much alive. She smiled and nodded at Erik. She wasn't sure what to say to him. She didn't know him well enough to say more. She decided that silence would be best. They finished looking at everything that the stall had to offer them. She was ready to leave it.

They went to pay for their purchases. Erik had seen her carefully looking at the chickadees and smiling. He could tell that she really liked them. When she reluctantly set them aside, he knew that he had to buy them for her because of her help today. He would either give it to her as they left the flea market or sometime soon afterward.

He looked at her and smiled sweetly. "Hey, what are you doing? I want to buy those cute chickadees," he said.

"You do? I didn't know that. I was just carrying them around while I decided whether or not to buy them," she said with surprise.

"Oh, yes, I want them. I thought that you were carrying them around for me. Grab them before someone else picks them up. They will make a cute addition to my collection. I love how they look so tenderly at each other," he said to surprise her.

She thought that she was the only one to see that expression on the chickadees. She smiled widely as she handed them over to him. If she couldn't have them, she was happy that Erik would have them in his collection.

They tiredly decided that they had enough great buys for the day. As they were slowly walking back to the entrance of the flea market, Melissa saw a lovely tapestry wall hanging depicting a mountain scene. It had a deep blue lake with a few deer next to it and an eagle in the light blue sky, surrounded by white-capped mountains. It was something that she instantly coveted, although it would not really go in her apartment, and it cost quite a lot of money.

"Oh, look at this, Erik. Isn't it lovely? I would love to buy this, but it wouldn't fit in with my current decor. Maybe I should buy it and put it away in case I want to totally remodel my apartment in the future," Melissa said excitedly.

Erik wished he could buy it for her, just because she loved it so much. However, they were barely friends at this point, and it would be inappropriate. He said to her, "I really like it, too. If you decide not to buy it, I will. It will look great on one of my walls."

Melissa thought about it for a second or two and regretfully said, "No, you take it. It's too lovely to sit in a closet until I decide to redecorate my apartment. You're right, it would look great in your place alongside the rest of the stuff you bought today."

He paid for it and asked them to hold on to it for him until he could come back for it. They walked out to his car and put his purchases in the back. She put the red cardinal for Susan's birthday carefully inside Sarah Rose's doll carriage. She walked back with him to pick up the tapestry. As they returned to their cars, they talked about their finds for the day. They both were very satisfied with their purchases.

Erik offered to follow Melissa home and carry her doll carriage up to her apartment for her. Melissa did not want to bother him, so she told him that she could manage it by herself. Erik thought that she was giving him the brush-off.

As she was opening her car door, he noticed for the first time that she had gotten quite sunburned. "I noticed that you got sunburned this afternoon. Are you okay? I feel bad. You walked around for hours in the sun helping me. Is there anything I can do for you?" he asked her anxiously.

Melissa looked with surprise at her arms and legs. She really had gotten quite burned. She usually knew better than to stay out so long in the sun. She had been enjoying her afternoon with Erik so much that she had not even thought about stopping and putting on some sun lotion. She noticed that his arms and legs looked burned, as well.

She made a slight grimace and said, "Thank you, Erik, but no, I'll be okay. Once I get home, I'll take a cool shower and put on some lotion. I should be fine. You look like you got sunburned, too. You should do the same."

He nodded and said, "Will you give me your phone number? I just want to call you later and make sure that you are okay."

His request surprised her. She nodded, and they exchanged phone numbers.

"Melissa, I can't thank you enough for all of your help, today. I can't wait to get home and arrange all these great buys in my living room. Take care of yourself, and make sure you do something about that sunburn, okay?" he asked her with an anxious look in his eyes.

"I had a fun time. I enjoy helping people decorate their homes. I have often thought that I could be an interior decorator on the side," she said with a warm smile. Erik saw the smile and had a difficult time not wrapping his arms around her and kissing her on those sweet-looking lips.

He walked her to her car, closed her door, waved at her, and walked away. In his concern over Melissa's sunburn, Erik forgot to give her the chickadees. *Oh, well,* he thought, *I'll give them to her the next time I see her.*

CHAPTER
SIX

When Melissa got home, she looked in the mirror and saw how bad her sunburn was. She took a nice cool shower and got into a loose sundress. She did not want anything to touch her burned skin. She tried to smooth lotion on all her burned skin, but some of her skin was hard to reach. She shook her head at her stupidity. She laid around until suppertime, just relaxing and sitting in a darkened room. She thought about Erik and all the things that she was starting to like about him. Her attraction to tall, large, muscular blond men went back a long way.

Melissa had loved watching the *Life and Times of Grizzly Adams* with her Grandpa Hillman. She saw it for the first time as an impressionable fourteen-year-old. She loved the character of Grizzly Adams, played by handsome actor Dan Haggerty. She loved his character, and because of that, loved his unique look. Thinking about her infatuation with the mountain man look made her smile even now. The fact that Grizzly Adams was a gentle and loving man who cared about nature and animals made her teenage crush even deeper. Her brother, Matt, used to tease her unmercifully about the giant-sized poster of Grizzly Adams that hung on the wall in her bedroom.

Then in high school, she fell for her Biology teacher. Mr. Miles was similar in appearance to Grizzly Adams and was passionate about the environment. He got so busy working on his many projects and organizations over the weekends that he would often come into school on Monday morning with a weekend's worth of scruffy stubble on his cheeks and chin. His whole shabby, disheveled, and casual look was very attractive to her. She had written "Mrs. Melissa Miles" on the inside of her Biology notebook that year. Even after meeting his petite wife, Melissa's crush on her teacher did not lessen. She finally outgrew it when she started dating.

Last year she ran into Mr. Miles and his wife at a Fun Fair. He remembered her since she had been such a good student and had spent many hours before and after class talking with him. He properly introduced Melissa to his wife, Houa, and their three daughters. The youngest one was about three years old and looked so happy snuggled up in her daddy's strong arms. The tenderness and love on Mr. Miles' face when he looked at his family left Melissa with a longing for that kind of marriage for herself one day. After some reflection, Melissa concluded that she was attracted to tall, large, blond men who had a gentle and loving soul.

She started to realize that Erik was someone she could really like. She already found him attractive; now she was starting to see the kind of man he was. Her initial dislike for him was quickly going by the wayside. He surprised her today with his deeply sensitive side.

At seven pm, someone buzzed to get into the apartment building. Speaking into the intercom, she asked who it was. "Hi, Melissa. It's Erik. I brought you something to make your sunburn feel better. Will you let me in to give it to you? It will only take a second," he said. His voice was upbeat and polite.

She buzzed him into the building. When he knocked on her door, she slowly and painfully moved to the door to let him in. Her skin was bright red by this time.

He looked at her and frowned. "Oh, Melissa, I am so sorry. You look like you are in terrible pain," he said in a worried voice.

He held out a tube of lotion and said, "My mom is a nurse. I told her about your sunburn. She told me to tell you that if you are really hurting, you should go to the clinic to get something to relieve your pain. Otherwise, if it's manageable, this lotion is good for sunburns. It relieves the pain and starts the healing process. Do you want to try it? Otherwise, I can take you to the clinic, if you want. She's working there tonight and would be happy to help you," he told her.

"Well, it does hurt, I guess. Maybe I should try your lotion first. If it doesn't help much, I'll go to the clinic. Thanks for bringing it," Melissa told him gratefully.

She took the lotion and started to carefully smooth it on her red skin. As she moved her arms, she involuntarily groaned from the pain in her burned shoulder muscles. Erik gently took the lotion from her and said, "Sit down, Melissa. Let me help you with that. Your shoulder muscles have tightened up, and I'll bet it hurts to move your arms. Now sit still while I put the lotion on for you."

He led her to the couch and sat her down. He very gently and carefully spread the lotion all over her shoulders and down her arms. He also rubbed some on the top of her head where the sun had burned her scalp.

"Lift up your skirt a little so I can get your knees and calves, too," he calmly instructed her. Melissa wasn't sure about that, but he was being so calm and matter of fact that she decided to let him continue to help her. There had been nothing even slightly sexual in his help thus far.

She lifted the skirt of her dress to show her knees. They were as red as her arms. Erik crouched down in front of her and gently spread the soothing lotion on her knees, calves, and feet. He told her to stand up so that he could get to the back sides of her legs. When he was done, her arms and legs felt so much better. The soothing ingredients in the lotion were already starting to take away some of the burn. Erik stood up and replaced the cap on the lotion. He put it on the kitchen table. For the first time, he looked around and wondered where the cat was.

"Where is Clarabelle?" he asked her.

"I put her in my bedroom. I couldn't bear her hot little furry body next to my skin. I think she sensed that I was hurting, and she kept trying to jump onto my lap and weave herself around my legs. I'll let her out when I go to bed. Then I'll close my door, so she stays out here and won't be able to climb up onto my bed," she explained to him.

"Good idea," he told her.

He looked at her and nodded. She looked better—not so much in pain. "Can I get you anything else?" he asked her.

"No, thank you, Erik. It is so nice of you to come over and help me. How about you? Your sunburn doesn't seem too bad," she remarked as she looked him over. *I suppose he never loses his base tan because he's outside so much*, she thought.

"I met Mom for supper. She gave me a tube of lotion to use for myself. I told her about you, and she gave me this extra tube for you. I'm fine. I think that I have a darker base tan than you had. I'm outside quite a bit."

Melissa inwardly grinned at the validation of her own musing. Erik, wiping his hands on a kitchen towel, continued, "I didn't get as much sunburn as you did. Again, I'm so very sorry that this happened to you. I guess that's one more strike against me, isn't it?" he asked somewhat sadly.

"No, Erik, don't blame yourself. I very much enjoyed my afternoon helping you find some great things to decorate your house. It was my own fault for not putting sunscreen on this morning. I knew that it was a hot sunny day. And it's not a strike against you. We're done being stupid about our first meeting. We've already resolved that, so don't even give it another thought," she firmly told him. Then, as if to emphasize her statement, she locked eyes with him and smiled broadly.

Erik nodded with relief. He smiled and, changing topics, told her, "I took pictures of my living room. Do you want to see how it looks after I put all of my new things in it?"

Melissa smiled happily and said, "I'd love to see them. Let me get us a couple of soft drinks and then we can sit down and look at the pictures, okay?"

They looked at his photos and commented on how much better the room looked with some color in it. She enjoyed looking at his house and seeing how he decorated the living room. She didn't see the tapestry, though.

"Where is the tapestry? I don't see it on any of the walls," she asked him in a puzzled voice.

"I haven't put it up yet. I'll need to get some brackets or a frame to put it up. I don't want to put nails into the fabric. Currently, it's rolled up on my bedroom floor. When I get it up on the wall, I'll take a picture of it and text it to you, okay?" he asked her.

"Great, I'll look forward to seeing it," she told him.

They talked for a little bit more until Erik said that he should get going. He asked her if she felt able to put more lotion on by herself. She blushed and told him that she could manage. He wondered why she was blushing but didn't comment on it.

When she walked him to the door, he put a gentle hand on her shoulder and said sincerely, "I'm glad you're okay. I was worried about you. Make sure you call me or someone if you need any help, okay? Good night, Melissa."

"Good night, Erik, and thanks for helping me tonight. Thank your mom for the lotion, okay?" she said as she opened the door. He nodded and then went into the hallway.

She quietly closed the door. Melissa sat down on her couch and thought over the evening. Erik had been wonderful. His gentleness as he smoothed on the lotion was remarkable. She liked the caring feel of his big hands applying lotion onto her skin. She still thought that he looked like a Viking, but today was the first time she realized just how handsome he was. He had such strong features. She found him to be very attractive, as well. She put more lotion on before she went to bed. Already, her sunburn was feeling so much better.

As Erik drove home, he thought about Melissa. He was glad that he brought her the lotion. His own sunburn felt much better, so hers probably did, too. He enjoyed their time together. He liked the feel of her soft smooth skin. She was an attractive girl, but more importantly, he was finding himself more attracted to her each time he was around her. He would have liked to kiss her, but he didn't dare. They did not have that kind of relationship yet. Because of her boyfriend, they probably never would, either.

He wanted to see her more often, but he also didn't want to start caring about her more than he already did. After the pain he went through when Diane and he had split up, he really did not want to feel any more pain on account of any woman. What's more, he reasoned, he never connected with Diane the way he was now connecting with Melissa. He did not want to cause Melissa any pain, ever.

He remembered the talk he had with his mom this afternoon. She wanted to know how he was doing without Diane. She knew about his vow to keep women out of his life. She was initially surprised when he talked about Melissa. She asked all the right questions, and he revealed everything about his bad start with Melissa. She asked him straight out if he liked her, and he had to admit that he did. He also told her that Melissa had a boyfriend, so at this point, there was no future in caring about her too much.

He remembered thinking to himself, *no matter how painful, this heartache is still better than a heart break.*

He went home and sat in his newly decorated living room and thought about Melissa some more until it was time for him to get some sleep. He would call her tomorrow, he decided. If she was totally okay, he would try to stay out of her way. Maybe he should stop volunteering at the house project. He saw her there more than at any other place. He should try to get on with his life.

Now that he knew that he was totally over Diane, he felt like he could start over with someone else. He would have liked that to be Melissa, but she had Brad. He had to let her go and hoped that he could rid himself of the caring he felt for her. *Tomorrow I'll open myself up to some new women*, he decided. He was glad that he had held off from giving her the chickadees. If he was going to stay away from her from now on, it was better if he didn't give them to her. They could sit on his bedroom dresser and keep him company.

The next day was Sunday. Melissa took herself off to her church. After church, she changed her good dress clothes for some comfy ones and took herself off to her parents' home for Sunday lunch. They were happy to see her but concerned about her sunburn. She was glad that the bright red from yesterday was already starting to fade. It didn't look as bad as it had yesterday.

She brought the doll carriage with her and told them that she bought it at the flea market. She did not mention Erik at all. They enjoyed their lunch and talked for a while. She asked them if she could keep the carriage at their place until the baby shower next Sunday. It would be held at Roy and Kay's home. Mark and Susan wanted Melissa to be at the shower, so they agreed to have it on Sunday. I was Melissa's Saturday to work at Tollie's.

Because of her sunburn, Melissa did not want to spend any time outdoors. She took herself home in the early afternoon. She was relaxing at home that afternoon when Erik called her.

"Hi, Melissa, this is Erik. I just called to see how you are doing. How is your sunburn? Does it feel any better today?" he asked her.

"Hi, Erik, Thanks for calling. Yes, I am feeling better today. I went to church this morning and to my parents' house for lunch. Now I am just relaxing at home. How about you? Is your sunburn doing okay, too?" she asked him.

"Yes, it's hardly even red, anymore. That lotion is good stuff. I am going to remember it in case I ever have a sunburn again," he said.

"Please thank your mom, again, for the lotion. It really helped me, too," Melissa said. She did not know what else to talk about, so silence reigned for a few seconds.

Erik also didn't know what to say. He was ready to say goodbye when Melissa said, "Did you know that Mark and Susan's baby shower is next Sunday at my parents' house? I know they planned to invite you."

"Yes, Mark called to invite me. Unfortunately, I'm out of town that day, and I won't be able to come. I plan to drop off my gift for baby Sarah sometime this week. I know that Susan is going to be thrilled with your doll carriage gift. I wish I could see you give it to her. Anyway, have a great time at the shower. I guess I'll see you at Tollie's in a few weeks, right? Have a great week, Melissa," he said regretfully, because it was going to be a long two weeks without seeing her.

Melissa was sad to hear that he was not going to be at the shower. She was looking forward to seeing him again. She said brightly, "Bye, Erik. See you at Tollie's."

As she hung up, she thought that it was quite ironic that she now actually wanted to see Erik. A month ago, she went out of her way to avoid him. Oh, well. He didn't seem to want to see her any sooner than their monthly meeting at the store. Maybe he really did not want to become friends with her. In that case, it was strange that he had come over last night to help her. His call today was considerate, too. *What is going on in his head?* she wondered.

The next day, Melissa received a surprise visitor at work. She had been in her office doing some paperwork. One of the cashiers knocked on her door. Melissa looked up and invited her in.

The cashier said, "Ms. Hillman, there is a woman who would like to see you. She said her name is Alison Lundstrom. May I bring her back here to meet with you?"

Melissa wondered if it could be Erik's mother for some reason. She was curious and said, "Yes, thank you for asking. Go ahead and bring her back here, please."

The cashier came back with a tall buxom blond woman with Erik's light blue eyes. Melissa stood up and smiled at her. She held out her hand to the woman. "Hello, Mrs. Lundstrom. I'm Melissa Hillman. How can I help you?" she asked the older woman.

Mrs. Lundstrom smiled at Melissa and shook her hand. She said, "Hello, Ms. Hillman, I came to help you." With that, she held out a tube of lotion. "My son told me about you and your sunburn. I thought that you might need some more lotion. It's not a very large tube, and it sounded like you had quite a burn."

Melissa took the tube from her and smiled. "Thank you so much. It really helped lessen the pain that I was feeling. I did use up the other tube, so I really appreciate you coming to give me another tube of it. Can I pay you for it?" she asked.

"No, no, I don't want any payment. From what Erik told me, you helped him so much. I have been after him to decorate that house of his ever since he bought it last year. He just never seemed to want to bother with it. He had other things on his mind, I guess," she said to Melissa.

Melissa liked this smiling Nordic woman who looked so much like Erik. She felt an immediate affinity for her. "I'm just about to go for lunch. Would you like to join me? We could talk for a little while longer then," she asked Erik's mom.

Alison Lundstrom looked pleased and said, "Thank you, Ms. Hillman. I have some time. I would enjoy talking with you some more. Where do you go for lunch?"

Melissa said, "I usually eat here in the lunchroom, but it's so nice outside that I thought that I would go and pick up something and eat outside in the shade. Does that sound okay to you?"

Alison said, "That sounds great. May I call you Melissa? Erik called you by that name, and it seems so much more friendly than Ms. Hillman. And I would love it if you called me Alison. I'll follow you in my car."

Melissa nodded and said that she would like that. She told the head cashier that she would be out for lunch for an hour and then led the way to her car. Alison followed her car to a deli that was close to the store. They chose their lunch and drove to a nearby park. They sat down at a picnic table that was in a shady spot. Because of her sunburn, Melissa did not want to sit in the direct sun just yet.

They spent a very nice hour talking about a variety of things. Melissa was surprised at how easy it was to talk to Alison. It was as easy as talking with her own mother. She also liked Alison's great sense of humor. She laughed at herself in a sweet way.

Alison talked about the difficulty of being a widow. Erik was their only child. Because of her husband's death, she and Erik were very close. They tried to meet for lunch or supper several times a week. She worked full-time as a Registered Nurse at the local clinic. Erik grew up in Litton. Their former family home was about ten miles from Erik's current house. Alison spoke briefly about Erik's old girlfriend, and Melissa had a distinct impression that Alison was glad that Diane and Erik had broken up. It seems that Diane had not been a good fit for Erik.

As Alison talked with her, she thought that Melissa was the perfect woman for her son. After knowing and barely tolerating Diane for a year or so, Alison found Melissa to be refreshingly intelligent, generous, and kind. Melissa was everything that Alison personally wanted to see in a daughter-in-law.

Alison had seen Erik's face light up when he talked about Melissa. He may not have been fully aware of his feelings for Melissa, but his mother knew him very well indeed. He deeply cared about Melissa, even though he stated regretfully that they could not be more than casual friends because she already had a boyfriend. Melissa and her boyfriend seemed inseparable whenever he had seen them together. *Oh, well, sometimes these things resolve themselves*, she thought.

"I really enjoyed meeting you, Alison. I hope that we will meet again, sometime," said Melissa sincerely. She shook Alison's hand and smiled.

Alison nodded and smiled back. "Me, too. Thank you for having lunch with me, Melissa. I'm glad that I came. I was curious to meet you. Erik has not talked about any woman since he broke up with Diane. He talked about you with such fondness. I'm glad that you and he can be friends. He needs that. He gets a little lonely sometimes. I know that he has a lot of male friends, but he needs some female friends, too—just to help smooth out his rough edges," she said with a smile as she thought about her son.

They said goodbye and went their separate ways.

Melissa thought about Alison and Erik quite a lot that afternoon when she was supposed to be working. Talking with his mom made her feel closer to Erik. Alison's interest in her son's happiness was reminiscent of Kay's involvement with her children. Melissa grinned as she recalled Kay's gentle persistence in getting her children to divulge their struggles. The grin widened as she imagined Alison "grilling" her Viking son under a bright light.

CHAPTER

SEVEN

Thursday evening after supper, Melissa and Brad dropped by Mark and Susan's house to see the baby. Because the baby was so new, Susan and Mark skipped the weekly basketball game at the Shelter. In Mark's absence, Paul directed the night's activities.

Brad and Susan had been friends in college. They had even dated casually before she married Mark. Brad had a cute gift for baby Sarah. Melissa helped him pick out an adorable pale pink dress, with ruffled tights, for Sarah at the mall. She wrapped it in cute paper and added lots of sparkles and a bow to the outside of the gift. *It looks very professionally wrapped—even if I say so myself,* she thought proudly.

They all were just sitting around on the deck when Erik came around the side of the house. He had a brightly wrapped gift in his hands. He looked at Melissa in surprise. She and Brad were sharing a big swivel chair. It was big enough for three people. It was Melissa's favorite chair, but Brad liked it, too, so they had squabbled about it and finally both sat down in it. To an outside observer's eyes, they looked cozy sitting in it together.

Melissa smiled at Erik. "Hi, Erik. It looks like we both had the great idea to stop by and see baby Sarah tonight." She looked at the gift in his hands and inquired, "Did you wrap your gift by yourself? Or did you have someone else wrap it for you?" She laughingly elbowed Brad because he had needed her help to wrap his gift.

Erik looked down at his gift and said ruefully, "Yeah, my mom wrapped it. I didn't ask her to do it, though. After I showed the gift to her, she offered to wrap it for me. I don't think she thought that I was talented enough to do it properly. I suppose you wrapped Brad's gift?"

"Of course. He's so hopeless at things like that," she jokingly told him. She smiled warmly at Brad to take the sting out of her declaration.

Brad gently patted her arm and shook his head at her. He said, "That's okay because I do lots of things better than Melissa, so it evens things out."

Erik didn't want to spend any more time watching Melissa and Brad. He turned to Mark and said, "I have to run. May I take a quick peek at Sarah and say hi to Susan? I only have a minute or two. I'm late for an appointment."

Mark said, "Sure, Erik. I'll take you inside to see them. I'm sorry that you don't have more time tonight. Stop by anytime for a longer visit."

Erik looked at Melissa and said, "It was good to see you both. Take care."

With that he followed Mark into the house, still carrying his gift. Melissa felt sorry that Erik had to leave so quickly. He had almost seemed abrupt. She hoped it wasn't because she was there. She was starting to wonder if he was trying to avoid her now.

As Erik drove home, he told himself that it was a good thing that he had decided to not seek out Melissa anymore. It looked as if she and Brad were close. He had to remember that. It was also a good thing that he had decided not to go to the baby shower. He would have had to see Melissa smiling and laughing at Brad the whole afternoon. *I don't think that I could bear that,* he thought unhappily.

That Sunday, the rain poured down so that the baby shower had to stay indoors. The house was crowded with guests and gifts. Melissa thought that Mark was being so sweet. He sat next to Susan and kept reaching over and kissing her hair, her hands, and her cheek. He held Sarah in the crook of his arm. He looked like the proudest papa that ever lived. He touched her tiny fingers and smoothed her dark hair in a sweet caress. It brought a lump to Melissa's throat. She wished with all her heart that she would someday have a baby and a husband who looked at her that way.

Mark and Susan received wonderful gifts for Sarah. Susan went into raptures over the doll carriage when Melissa presented it to them. She was glad that she had spent the extra money to get something that she just knew they would love.

It was a truly lovely afternoon. Melissa felt so close to her family, now. She thought back to three years ago. At that time, Mark was still in New York, and their family was not close at all. She felt blessed to have such a wonderful family life now.

The week after the baby shower was a busy one for Melissa at work. On Friday afternoon, Erik walked into the store. Melissa was in her office getting caught up on some paperwork. He peeked his head around the corner of her open door. She looked up and smiled warmly at him. Her smile made Erik's heart ache. He had decided to stay away from her, but it hadn't helped. He thought about her all the time. He knew now that he cared deeply for her. If Brad had not been an issue, he would have wanted to start dating her.

He smiled and asked her, "Are you busy? Do you have time to go over your order with me? If you're too busy, just send your order to me through email, okay?" He looked quizzically at her.

Melissa looked at him and said, "No, I can talk. I can finish this stuff up later. Come in and sit down, Erik."

His large body barely fit into the small chair that was in front of her desk. It looked quite uncomfortable for him. He took up so much room in her tiny office that she decided to take him into the staff lounge. They didn't have anything confidential to talk about, anyway.

She stood up and told him, "Let's go into the staff lounge to talk, if you don't mind." She was trying to give him a more comfortable seat, but Erik thought that she did not want him in her office for some reason. Maybe she did not want to be alone with him. They were totally at cross purposes with each other, unfortunately.

He nodded okay. He resigned himself for a very quick meeting with her. It only took about ten minutes to go over the new order. When they finished, Erik looked like he was getting ready to get up and leave.

Melissa wanted to keep him talking for a few more minutes, so she asked him, "Did you ever get that tapestry hung? You never sent me the text, so I didn't know if you had done it or not." She looked at him with a small smile.

Erik was surprised at her question but answered quickly, "No, it's still rolled up on my bedroom floor. I have been too busy to get to the hardware store and buy a frame for it. I promise that I will take a photo of it when it is hung and send it to you."

He smiled and rose to his feet, anxious to get out of there. Melissa felt his desire to get away and felt bad about it. It really did seem that Erik was avoiding spending any time with her. She tried to think of a reason for it but could not. She stood up, too. She held out her hand to him and said coolly, "Thank you for stopping by, Erik. I guess I will see you next month, okay?"

He held her hand for a second and nodded. "Thanks for your time, Melissa. I'll see you next month," he responded just as coolly as she had. He walked out of the store. Melissa watched him go and felt sad at his obvious reluctance to spend any extra time with her.

*　*　*

Melissa went to the construction site of the second project house the next Saturday that she was not working at Tollie's. She hoped to see Erik there. Brad couldn't come with her that day, so she went by herself. When she got there, she saw Erik right away. He was standing with his arm around a new volunteer. She was about thirty-five, and she seemed nice. Melissa liked her immediately.

Erik smiled at Melissa and introduced the two women. "Greta, this is Mark's sister, Melissa. Melissa, meet Greta Brown. She has promised to volunteer whenever she can make it. Her eight-year-old son is around here somewhere, too. His name is Tommy," he said cheerfully.

Melissa and Greta smiled at each other and shook hands. Mark came over and asked Melissa to show Greta around the site. Then he asked them to start painting one of the walls. Melissa got enough paint and supplies for them both. As they worked, Melissa asked Greta about herself and how she knew about the project.

"I just met Erik on Monday. He is the food rep for the grocery store where I work. We talked for a while in the store. Then he asked me if I wanted to get a cup of coffee after my shift at the store. I told him that I had to get home to my son. He said to bring him with us, so I went home, got Tommy, and met him at the local coffee shop. He was so great with Tommy. I've been divorced for a few years, and usually, men run far away when they know that I have a son. Not Erik, though. It didn't seem to bother him a bit. We went out again on Wednesday. He told me about his volunteer work here. I like to give back to the community, so I said I would come and help. I sometimes work on Saturdays, so I won't be able to volunteer every Saturday. It's kind of fun, getting to meet new people, isn't it?" she asked Melissa.

Melissa agreed with her. It seemed that Erik had found himself a girlfriend. *Maybe that is why he doesn't want to hang around me,* she thought. *No, wait, he only met Greta on Monday. He has been avoiding me for longer than that. It must just be my personality.* That contemplation saddened her.

She thought that they were becoming friends, especially after that Saturday at the flea market. He had been so sweet about helping her with her sunburn, too. Why had he suddenly changed? She wished that she could ask him. Now, it seemed as if it was too late. Great, just when she started to get interested in getting to know Erik better, he decided to start avoiding her. *Life is not fair sometimes,* she thought sadly.

During their lunch break, Erik went to get Tommy from wherever he was working. He put Tommy on his big shoulders and walked around with him. He met Melissa and Greta at the buffet table. He set Tommy down and helped him get a plateful of food.

He looked at Greta and Melissa and asked them, "Where do you girls want to sit? Is the picnic table okay with you?" He looked specifically at Greta and raised his eyebrows. She told him that the picnic table would be fine. He said, "I'll get Tommy over there and save you girls some seats." His smile included Melissa.

For two cents Melissa would have declined and sat with Matt and Tessa, but she felt like Greta would be hurt if she left her. After all, they were partners on the construction site today. Melissa filled her plate and followed them to the picnic table. She sat down. It was difficult to sit there watching Erik gently flirt with Greta and spend a lot of time with Tommy.

Erik barely spoke to Melissa, although he acted friendly enough toward her. Her appetite deserted her. She barely ate a thing, which was something that Erik saw and was concerned about. As soon as she could, Melissa excused herself and said she wanted to visit a little bit with her brothers. She walked away and threw her lunch in the trash.

She knew that she was laughing too much and too loudly because Matt and Mark kept looking at her quizzically and thoughtfully. They recognized Melissa's nervous trait as a defense mechanism when she was upset about something.

She was glad to go back to work. She maintained a friendly attitude with Greta but did not ask her any more personal questions. Greta seemed to sense that Melissa did not want to talk, because she stopped chatting, as well. They finished their painting in friendly silence.

When they were wrapping up, Melissa waved to Erik and Tommy, told Greta how happy she was to meet her, and took herself off to talk with Matt. She had planned to go to the recreation center with everyone that evening, but now she just needed to get away from Erik and Greta.

She lied and told Matt, "I know that I said that I was going to the rec center, but I got a call while I was painting. Is it okay with you if I skip it tonight? I have a date. Will you guys be hurt if I go on this date? I really want to go out tonight." She looked hopefully at Matt.

He teased her about preferring a date over her brothers but said she should go. She hugged him and told him to kiss Tessa from her. She got into her car and drove home. As she fixed herself some supper she thought, *Oh, no, not this again.* Lately, it seemed as if she was leaving her family gatherings just to get away from Erik. Only now it wasn't because she hated him; it was because she liked him.

What a waste of a Saturday night. Now she was stuck at home by herself, just because she didn't want to see Erik flirt with Greta. She picked up Clarabelle and cuddled her. Here she was, sitting there alone in her darkened living room, stroking her cat. *What a life I have,* she thought unhappily.

Erik was concerned about Melissa. She had barely eaten anything, and she had left so abruptly. He wondered what was wrong. He overheard Matt tell Mark that Melissa had begged off meeting everyone at the rec center because she wanted to go on a date, instead. Erik's lips pursed. Here he was, in the presence of a perfectly nice woman and her son, and he was upset that Melissa left to go on a date. He liked Brad well enough, but right now he was quite jealous of Brad's relationship with Melissa. Oh, well, he would have to try harder to get interested in Greta. She was so nice.

The next Thursday night at the Shelter's basketball game, Melissa saw Erik with Greta and Tommy. Erik was introducing them to the other kids and Shelter supporters. His arm was around Greta's shoulders and he had a hand on top of Tommy's blond head. They looked like a loving family to Melissa. She felt a bitter taste in her mouth when she looked at them and chastised herself for feeling the way she did. After all, she should be happy for Erik that he found a nice woman to be in his life.

Ever since she spoke with Erik's mom, Melissa wondered if she could be that female friend in his life. It didn't mean that they had to have a great romance, it was just that she liked him and would like to get to know him even better. She could further help him decorate his home, too.

Melissa decided that she and Erik were destined to never be more than very casual friends. Oh, she saw him often enough, but it always seemed as if there was still some barrier between them. She supposed that it was her fault. After all, she had cut him dead for two months after their first meeting. Although he had formally apologized, he was probably still wary of her and did not want to take the time to really get to know her.

He had kindly driven her home after the picnic, and she had enjoyed their time together at the flea market. She could still remember how caring his big hands had felt when they smoothed lotion on her burning skin. As pleasant as those recollections were to her, it now seemed as if Erik had found not one, but two, with whom to create new memories.

Well, Melissa concluded to herself, *I will try to be as friendly as I can be and not let him see that his relationship with Greta hurts me in any way.* Melissa smiled wryly to herself. *Easier said than done!* Still, Greta was really nice. She and Tommy deserved someone nice like Erik to help them and befriend them. *It was probably young Tommy's dream come true,* she thought.

"Hi, Greta and Tommy. Hi, Erik. It sure is a great evening for a basketball game, isn't it?" Melissa brightly asked them. She smiled at all three of them.

"Hi, Melissa. Couldn't Brad make it, tonight?" asked Erik as he looked around him.

"No, he had other plans tonight. How have all of you guys been?" Melissa asked the group.

Greta smiled and said, "Erik wanted Tommy to meet some of the kids who play basketball on Thursday nights. Tommy has been wanting to learn how to play. It's really nice to meet so many great people." She had her hand in Erik's. He smiled at her and squeezed her hand.

He nodded and said, "Yes, why not? The more kids, the better. This is such a good activity for them. Tommy will really love playing with these guys. They're a fun group of kids."

He looked at Melissa and asked, "How has the job been going? The last time I was there, it seemed that the store was full of people. Are sales going well?"

Melissa thought it was sad that the only thing they seemed to be able to talk about was work. She smiled nicely at Erik and said, "Yes, it has been very busy all week. I almost considered calling you and making an extra order this week."

"Sure, you can do that. Call me tomorrow if you need to order any more products," he said with a friendly smile for her.

Melissa couldn't think of anything else to say, so she just said to the group, "Well, have fun tonight. I need to talk with Sarah for a little bit. Please excuse me." With a bright forced smile and a wave, she turned around and made her way over to Sarah.

Greta looked closely at Erik. He watched Melissa's departure without any expression. He saw her walk over to sit by Sarah. He didn't realize that he was staring at her, but he continued to watch

Melissa for the next five minutes. In that five minutes, a look of longing crossed his face that he had no knowledge of; Greta was sure of that.

Greta wondered if Erik liked Melissa. It seemed as if he did. From her vantage point, it seemed as if they both liked each other but were concealing their true emotions for some reason. She wondered why.

She liked Erik. He was kind to Tommy and her. Yet, she always felt that he held something back. It seemed as if he was hurting. He told her briefly that he and his old girlfriend broke up a year ago. She had wondered if his reserved nature was caused by that. But now she knew that he was holding back from really getting to know her because he had unresolved feelings for Melissa. Greta wasn't in love with him. It was just nice to have a male friend and someone for Tommy to look up to.

Melissa tried to keep her eyes and mind focused on the game as she sat with Sarah and Tessa. Susan had stayed home with the baby tonight. She sat there, not contributing anything to the conversation as Sarah and Tessa talked about Erik. Although this was not an easy task, Melissa did her best to show more interest in the game than in the discussion at hand.

It seems that Erik had taken Greta and Tommy to several events that Sarah and Tessa had also attended. Tessa was speculating whether Erik was in love with Greta. They talked about young Tommy and how nice it would be for him if Erik married Greta. Melissa did not know why that idea hurt her so much. After all, she and Erik were barely friends.

As soon as the game was over, she hugged her brothers and told them that she had to get going. She brightly told them that she had a very busy day the next day and had some planning to do. They were disappointed, but they all knew what work pressures were like, so they let her go without saying too much. As she walked to her car, she waved gaily to Greta, Tommy, and Erik, who were just walking towards Matt and Tessa. She saw them wave back to her.

She went home and sat watching TV, too upset to eat any supper. She had not felt hungry for a week or more. It had been a struggle to eat something each evening. She wondered what was causing her lack of appetite.

The next evening, Melissa stopped in to eat supper with her parents. Matt, Tessa, Mark, Susan, and the baby were also there. They had a nice meal. Mark and Matt teased Melissa unmercifully about her preferring to go on dates rather than spending time with her family. Melissa laughingly teased them back about being more boring than her dates.

That got everyone asking her about her most recent date. On the spot, she had to invent a guy named Jeffrey. She told them that she had met him through Brad. It all sounded very plausible to them. They had absolutely no idea that she liked Erik. She planned to keep it that way, too.

While the men watched some sports on the television, Melissa sat in the kitchen with all the ladies. She listened to their cheerful chatter but didn't have much to contribute. She had no idea that her face looked quite sad.

Her mom, who had deep insights into her children's emotions, watched her and wondered why Melissa was so sad. If she wasn't mistaken, she thought that Melissa was in love and unhappy about it. She had seen that same expression on both of her sons' faces before they got married. Yet Melissa rarely went out. True, she went out with her friend, Brad, quite a lot. Then there was this new guy, Jeffrey, that Melissa had just told them about. But somehow

Kay did not think it was either of those two men. No, her Melly was unhappy and trying not to show it. Kay could bide her time. She would let Melissa know that she was available, in case she wanted to talk about it.

CHAPTER
EIGHT

The next week Melissa got a call from Matt asking her if she was available to come over on Saturday evening. It was her Saturday to work at Tollie's, but she would be done at five pm. He stressed that it would be a family dinner party. She agreed to be there by six o'clock. He teased her that she had better not break her promise because she wanted to go on a date. She promised to come.

It was a busy week at the store. Sales had been booming. She kept thinking of calling Erik to put in an extra order, but she decided against it. She would give it another week to see what the sales looked like.

She was tired by the time she got off work Saturday evening. She went home and took a revitalizing shower. As she stood in the shower, she noticed that she had lost some weight. It wasn't surprising—they had been crazy busy at the store, and she had not been eating right, either.

She looked through her closet and found an old dress that she had always loved. It had been a bit too tight for her the last few years. Now the dress fit her perfectly, again. The cobalt blue color looked lovely with her dark curling hair, blue eyes, and impressive tan. It emphasized her newly svelte figure, too. She left her hair hanging in loose curls instead of putting it into her usual ponytail. Because she wanted to boost her morale, she wore the diamond earrings that her parents had given her for her college graduation. She was very satisfied with her appearance when she looked in the mirror. *Too bad I am wasting this nice outfit on my family,* she thought with a sigh.

When she arrived, her mom, Tessa, and Susan all exclaimed at how pretty she looked. Even her dad and brothers told her that she looked nicer than usual. She laughingly thanked them.

Tessa looked radiant tonight. Her cheeks were flushed, and she was wearing a new and very pretty dress. She tended to wear jeans and button-down shirts just around the family. They sat down to a tasty Italian dinner. Tessa's favorite food was anything Italian. Because it was her favorite type of food, she made it quite often, and so she was an expert in its preparation. After the meal, they sat around the table and talked generally for a few minutes before the ladies started to clear the table. Melissa couldn't help but notice that Tessa and Matt kept looking at each other. They were using some kind of sign language between themselves, but Melissa couldn't figure it out.

Finally, Matt said loudly, "Hey, everyone, can we have your attention for a minute?"

Everyone stopped talking and looked expectantly at him. He took Tessa's hand in his, looked at her tenderly, and said, "We wanted you all to know that we're having a baby. We're so thrilled about it."

Everyone shouted, "Congratulations!" There were huge smiles on the faces of everyone there. They hugged and kissed Matt and Tessa with so much joy.

Matt pulled Tessa into a gentle hug, and they both turned to look at everyone. They said that Tessa was three months pregnant. The baby was due around Valentine's Day next year. There was a lot of excited talk for the next half hour.

Finally, Melissa and her mom cleared the table and started doing the dishes. Susan was feeding the baby and Tessa was still talking with the others. This gave Kay the perfect opportunity to talk privately with Melissa.

"How are you doing, honey?" Kay asked Melissa. She looked intently at Melissa as she asked it. Melissa saw her look and knew that the inquisition was about to begin.

"I'm doing fine, Mom," Melissa told her quietly.

"You've lost some weight. Have you been feeling alright?" Kay asked with a concerned look.

"Mom, I'm fine. It has been a very busy week for me. You know I can't eat when I'm under stress," Melissa tried to assure her.

"I know, honey, but you have been looking sad for a few weeks now. You look like your brothers did when they first fell in love," Kay told her.

Melissa was shocked. It wasn't until that very moment that she realized that she was in love, and it was with Erik. How could that be? They had hardly spent any time at all together.

Kay saw her shocked look and realized that she had been right. Her little Melly was in love, but she hadn't known it until that moment.

"Do you want to talk about it, Melly?" Kay asked her daughter very gently.

Melissa's eyes filled with tears. She turned to look at her mom. She really did want to talk with someone about it. Her mom was always very discreet about anything that Melissa shared with her. However, she didn't want to bawl at tonight's party. It was Tessa and Matt's big night.

Melissa hugged her mom and said, "I do want to talk with you, Mom, but not tonight. This is Matt and Tessa's night. I don't want to be crying while everyone is here. May I come to lunch tomorrow and then tell you about it when Dad watches the game on TV?"

Kay hugged Melissa tightly and said, "Of course, honey. Your dad plans to watch the game from two o'clock until about three-thirty or four o'clock. We'll go for a drive and you can tell me then. I won't say anything more, because I don't want you to keep crying. You're right, Matt and Tessa should have tonight all for themselves, without having to share it." She kissed Melissa and said, "Okay, let's start on these dishes. Maybe we can get them done quickly."

Melissa dried her tears and pulled herself together. They finished all the dishes and went back into the living room to hang out with the others. An hour later, most of them were sitting around the table playing a card game. Matt and Tessa were getting out more snacks and cold beverages.

Mark asked Matt, "What are you doing, bro?"

Matt smiled at everyone at the table and told them, "We asked some of our friends to come around for a while for drinks and to play cards. We'll tell everyone about the baby then. You are welcome to stay or go home, but we really hope that you will all stay. It will be more fun with all of you here."

Melissa was invested in the card game that she was playing, so she stayed in her seat behind the table. Her eyes were still a bit red from her earlier tears, but her family was still so excited about the baby news that they did not even notice. She looked up abruptly when Erik and two other volunteers from the Shelter came in the door. She smiled sweetly at them. They sat down at the table and said hello to everyone there.

Erik looked at Melissa and thought about how beautiful she looked. Because he looked at her so intently, he saw that she had been crying. He knew for a positive fact at that moment that he loved her. He felt sad that she was hurting about something. After her first smile at him, she looked down at the cards in her hands. She had not looked up since then. Her black lashes on her flushed cheeks looked lovely. Erik tried not to stare at her because anyone could see him doing so. He did not want to cause anyone to question him about her. He tried to look around at other people, but his gaze kept coming back to look at her beautiful face.

He looked at Matt and Tessa when they told everyone about the baby. He was so pleased for them. He had learned to really like this whole family during the last three or four months. He heard himself tell Matt congratulations even while his brain was trying to wrap around the idea that he loved Melissa. He just wanted to go somewhere quiet and think about it.

He had never felt this kind of love before. His relationship with Diane had been more physical and less emotional. While he had crushes on women before, he had never loved them the way he loved Melissa. Erik felt like hitting something because of the unfairness of life. Melissa was dating Brad. He didn't know how serious they were, but he would not try to break them up. To do that would make him into a jerk. He just had to hope and pray that she would break up with Brad and realize that she liked him, instead.

The card game ended, and Matt declared new partnerships for the next game. He declared that whoever was sitting directly across from each player would now be their new partner. That made Melissa Erik's partner. He was a pretty competitive guy. He looked directly at Melissa, smiled into her eyes and said, "Melissa, I play to win. Let's wipe the floor with these chumps, okay?"

Melissa's eyes began to twinkle as she said, "You're on, partner. Let's beat these guys. I hope you know how to play this game." She smiled brightly at him.

It turned out that they both were competitive card players. They paid more attention to the game than some of the others and won the game by a large margin. Erik was enchanted by Melissa's quick wit and intelligent card playing. He watched her expressive face and pretty hands. How he wished that she was his girlfriend. He had a difficult time not grabbing her and hugging her. He wanted above all things to kiss her with all the passion he felt for her.

Meanwhile, he had no idea that he was being watched closely by Kay Hillman. She was not playing cards but was sitting nearby watching the game. She also watched Melissa's face light up when she talked with Erik. *Here, then, is the man that my little Melly is in love with*, Kay concluded, with a certainty that only a mother could possess.

Kay wondered what the problem was. They both seemed to love each other so much. Why couldn't they just tell each other so? However, she remembered all the anguish and troubles that her sons had with their love lives. She also remembered that tonight Tessa had been talking about Erik and someone named Greta. Tessa thought that Erik was in love with Greta. She said that Greta had a young son who was becoming very attached to Erik. There apparently had to be some misunderstanding somewhere. Kay determined that she was going to have to somehow rectify this situation. *Why not?* she thought. *I've managed to nudge both of my sons toward happiness, haven't I?*

After they won their game, Melissa and Erik got up from the table to stretch. They exchanged a modest high-five. They left the table so that someone else could sit down in their places and play the next game. When Melissa went around the corner of the living room into the kitchen to get a beverage, Erik followed her. He noticed that Melissa had lost some weight. Her dress clung lovingly to her curves. *She really looks lovely tonight,* he thought to himself.

She asked him what he wanted to drink. Because he would be driving soon, he told her to get him a soft drink. She took one as well. They moved back into the living room, which was so crowded that they decided to go out into the backyard. It was a nice evening. The stars were out, and the pine trees scented the backyard nicely.

There were a few other people sitting on chairs around the patio table. Melissa sat down next to one of the other volunteers from the Shelter. Erik took a seat in the first chair that he could find closest to Melissa. Since the setting afforded no privacy, he could not talk privately with her. He had to content himself just being in the same area as Melissa and watching her while she chatted with others.

Erik briefly wished that he was an unscrupulous man who could try to cut Brad out without a worry. He knew that he could not do that, but he nevertheless wished that Brad would just go away. He wanted his chance with Melissa. If he ever got that chance, he would make darned sure that he never messed things up. He would give her the moon if she wanted it.

After an hour of light conversation, Melissa stated that she had to get going. The party was starting to break up, anyway. Erik made his excuses to Matt and walked out to his car at the same time as Melissa and a few others. He touched her shoulder and quietly said goodnight to her. He waved to the others before getting in his car and driving away.

As he drove home, Erik thought about the fact that he loved Melissa. He did not see how he could move forward until Melissa either broke up with Brad or married him. He loved to see her and be in her presence, but it hurt him knowing that she apparently loved Brad. Nothing good could come out of hanging around her, given the current set of circumstances.

He liked Greta and Tommy, but they were just friends. He still wanted to take them out and about, but he was going to have to tell Greta that there was no future for them as a couple. He could never be with her if there was a chance that he could have Melissa. He would only give up any hope for a life with Melissa when she married someone else.

It seemed that he would just have to wait and see what happened. In the meantime, he could spend some of his free time helping others. And someone who needed lots of help was Tommy. That little boy was too shy and awkward. He needed friends and a male role model in his life. With that last thought, he went home and went to bed.

As Melissa drove home, she thought about Erik. She had felt so shocked when her mom told her that she acted like she was in love. *How did Mom know?* she wondered. She wondered if anyone else could see it. She hoped not—that would be a very embarrassing situation for her. She now knew why she had been so unhappy lately and why she had been hurt when she saw the closeness between Erik and Greta.

She thought about this evening. Erik had been so charming and fun tonight. She had approved of his card-playing and witty conversation while they played the game. However, he had been so quiet when they were sitting on the patio. She could never tell what he was thinking.

She wondered, again, about his relationship with Greta. She would just have to wait and see what happened. Maybe he was not in love with her. Melissa would watch carefully and wait to see if she could ever have a chance with him. She could just imagine what it would feel like to have his strong arms around her, holding her close to him. With that thought, she went to bed.

As soon as Melissa got home from church the next morning, her phone rang. It was Brad. He was calling to see if he could talk with her. She told him that she had been invited for lunch at her parents' home. He told her that it would only take a few minutes. She told him that if he came over right away, she could give him fifteen minutes or so. She quickly changed her clothes before he arrived. She wanted to be able to fly out of the door as soon as their conversation ended.

"Hi, Melly. How are you?" Brad asked her as soon as she opened the door to him. Melissa was surprised. He seemed to be looking at her so intently.

"Come in, Brad. Do you want a soft drink?" she asked him before answering his question.

"No, I know that you don't have much time. Let's sit down for a minute, though," he said.

They sat down on the couch. He looked at her with concern on his face. She looked back and wondered why he was there.

She said, 'I'm fine, Brad. What do you want to talk about?"

Brad took hold of one of her hands and said gently to her, "Melly, I am your best friend. I have been worried about you. You have been sad and distant for the last several weeks. It's obvious that you haven't been eating because you've lost weight. You have always told me your troubles in the past, but lately, you have shut me out. Every time I ask you how you are, you say you're fine. I know that you're not fine. I really want you to tell me what is wrong. You never know, I might be able to help you. We've always been there for each other. Let me help you now." He looked at her with love as he spoke.

Melissa thought about all the problems that they had gone through together in the last four years. Brad was a very good friend. Maybe he could help her in some way. She started to quietly tell Brad about her problem.

"Brad, I just realized last night that I am in love with someone who doesn't love me back. I was talking with Mom last night, and she asked me about it, and I had to finally admit it," she sadly told him.

Brad looked a little surprised and cautiously asked her, "Melly, I didn't even know that you were dating anyone. What happened, and who are you in love with?"

Melissa asked with effort, "You know Erik Lundstrom, right?"

Brad said, "Sure, the big guy who volunteers at the construction site and plays basketball at the Shelter. I thought that you hated him for saying something unkind to you when you first met. Why? Is he the guy you love?"

Melissa told him everything. She had already told him months ago about that first disastrous meeting. Now she told him about everything that had happened since. She cried bitterly as she told him.

Brad thought back to the times that he had been hanging around with Melissa, and they had met up with Erik. He had to agree that Erik had never seemed to want to get to know her better.

It had always seemed like Erik was abrupt with Melissa. Brad pulled her into a tight hug. He had been in love before. He knew how much it hurt when the one you loved didn't love you back.

Melissa tearfully said, "I would die if Erik guessed how I feel about him. I try so hard not to watch him when we are at the same event. I don't want anyone to guess. The problem is, he is good friends with everyone in my family. I can't avoid seeing him unless I stop spending time with them."

Brad shook his head no and said, "Melly, you can't stop spending time with your family. You have often told me how happy you are that you've all become so close these last few years. You can't give that up, now. Are you sure about his relationship with Greta and Tommy? Could you be mistaken about that?"

Melissa said, "I've seen them together three or four times. He always has his arm around her, and he spends quite a lot of time with Tommy. Besides, Tessa and Susan told me that they have seen Erik and Greta together a lot, too. Greta is such a nice person. She deserves to have a man who will treat Tommy and her well. In the times that I have seen them together, they seemed like a family unit. Erik is so loving toward them. I don't want to mess up anything for Greta. Oh, Brad, what am I going to do?" she cried.

"Well, Melly, maybe you and I should crank it up. Whenever you go to an event that Erik will be at, I will be there with you. Let him think that we are a couple," he suggested.

"But Brad, my family knows that we're just best friends. We wouldn't be able to fool them," she protested.

"Well, Melly, we don't have to fool your family, we just have to make Erik and Greta think that we are dating. I very much doubt that he will ask your brothers about me. What do you think? Do you want to try it? I'm game if you are," Brad said with firm friendship.

"Okay, Brad, we can try it for a few events. We can watch what happens with Erik and Greta while we are at it," she told him.

Melissa felt strange planning to deceive Erik and Greta, but it was better than allowing anyone to guess that she had feelings for him. Melissa and Brad talked for a few more minutes. She felt marginally better, knowing that she had a plan and that Brad would help her through this mess. She told him that she had to go, and he reluctantly left. She drove to her parents' house and wondered how much she should tell her mom.

When she got to her parents' home, Melissa sat for a minute in her car while she thought about how to tell her mom about Erik. Her mom was perceptive and could always tell when her children were lying or keeping things from her. It would be comforting to tell her mom. That way, she would have someone to talk to about Erik.

She loved Brad, but he was a man. He would not really understand what she was going through. Oh, she knew that he had been in love before, but he would look at the situation from a man's point of view. *Yes, it is probably best for me to tell Mom,* she concluded. *Who knows when I may need her support?*

Melissa had a very nice lunch with her parents. As her dad went into the living room to watch the game on television, Melissa told him that she and Kay were quickly going to the store. He nodded and waved goodbye to them. *He was already thinking about the game,* Melissa thought. Her dad always seemed oblivious to anything going on with his kids. Her mom was the total opposite. She was so in tune with all their feelings and emotions. *Mom is totally amazing,* thought Melissa.

They got into Kay's car, and she drove to the local supermarket. She parked the car in the last place in the parking lot. As she turned to look at Melissa, Kay remembered coming to this exact spot to talk with each of her sons when they were going through a tough time before they married their wives. She inwardly grinned. *This is getting to be a habit,* she thought. She looked at Melissa with love and raised eyebrows. "Do you want to start, Melly, or should I tell you what I have observed?" she asked quietly.

Melissa was not really very surprised. Her mom had surprising powers of deduction. "Why don't you tell me what you have observed, Mom, and I'll tell you if you are on the right track?" she asked her mom, just as quietly.

Kay thought for a moment before she started speaking. Then she looked lovingly at Melissa as she said, "Honey, I have watched you getting sadder and sadder these last few weeks. You've stopped eating, and you probably feel like no one in the world could ever feel the way you feel. Am I right?" she asked her daughter.

Melissa nodded and said, "Yes, that is exactly the way I have been feeling. Only I didn't know that I was in love until you said something yesterday. I really had no idea why I was so unhappy for weeks. When you said that I was acting like Mark and Matt had acted when they were in love, I was shocked to find out that I was feeling that way, too. I remember them when they thought that their love for Susan and Tessa was hopeless. I'm feeling that same way, I guess."

Kay said, "I kept wondering who you could be in love with. I knew it wasn't Brad because he is just your best friend. And I knew it wasn't this Jeffrey guy that you just told us about. There was no spark in your eyes when you talked about him. No, it was last night that I figured out who it was. It's Erik Lundstrom, isn't it, Melly?"

Melissa's jaw dropped as she thought, *how could she possibly know that?* "Mom, how did you know? I never talked about him with you. I never talked about him with anyone," she asked in a shocked voice.

Kay smiled at her and picked up Melissa's hand. She said lovingly, "I watched you when he came over last night. Every time you looked at him or talked to him while you were playing cards, your whole face lit up. You tried very hard not to let anyone see how you felt, but I'm your mother. I love you, and I know you. I can tell when you are unhappy and when you are glad. You haven't looked that way for weeks. Then, suddenly, you had joy back in your face. I was so happy to see that but also concerned. I knew that you wouldn't tell him for some reason. Why, honey?" She shook Melissa's hand gently.

"Oh, Mom. I think that he is in love with a woman named Greta Brown. Greta has a little boy who loves and needs Erik. He is a little cutie but so shy and awkward. He looks at Erik with such hero worship on his face. And Greta is a very nice woman. She has had such a raw deal with her ex-husband. She deserves someone like Erik in her life. While I love Erik and want him for myself, I would never try to take him away from them. I see them together, and they look like a family to me. If he loves them, I want him to marry Greta, and they can all be a happy family."

Here, Melissa paused, half relieved to be finally telling her mom and half devastated to hear herself say those last words. She inwardly questioned herself, *Really? Do I really want Erik to marry Greta?*

She looked at her mom with eyes that seemed to beg for an answer, any answer that was better than the one she was contemplating. Kay's maternal gaze remain fixed on her daughter, yet she said nothing at this point. She knew that Melissa needed to unburden herself in the comfort of a mother's understanding. Kay also firmly believed in her children's ability to find the answer, given time and support. For parents, that sometimes meant saying little, but loving much.

Melissa, gathering her thoughts in the lull, took a breath and continued, "I know about his terrible breakup with his old girlfriend. He has hated women for a year. Now he finally looks happy, again. I would never mess up anything between them just to get him for myself. I guess that it's true when people say that when you love someone, you want their happiness more than you want your own."

She looked at her mom, tears falling down her face. It felt so good to talk to someone about her feelings. Even though she was crying, she felt a huge weight being lifted off her shoulders.

Kay hugged Melissa tightly and just let her cry until she was cried out. She knew that Melissa would be able to deal with this situation better after she had really come to terms with all of it. She felt proud of Melissa for putting Erik's feelings before her own. She also felt proud of her loving and caring daughter for taking Greta and Tommy's feelings into account.

"Mom, I need you to promise me that you will not tell anyone, not even Dad, about my love for Erik. I need to process everything in my mind before I could ever tell my brothers. You see, they all like Erik and are friends with him. I don't want them to feel differently toward him just because I'm unhappy. No, I need to deal with it myself. I know that Mark and Susan and Matt and Tessa love me. They would try to find a way to tell Erik or something like that. I would absolutely die if he found out, and he loved Greta. If that ever happened, Mom, I would have to leave here. Remember Mark and his disastrous love affair with Valerie? Well, he left Litton for fourteen years. We barely saw him during that time. If Erik ever found out, and he was either engaged or married to someone else, I would not stay in Litton. I really mean that, Mom. You have to promise that you will say nothing about this to anyone," Melissa implored plaintively.

Kay hugged her again and said, "I promise, Melly. I will not tell anyone about what you and I have just talked about. But I want you to know that I am here for you. If you ever want to talk to me some more about anything, please call me and let me know. Or better still, drop by and we'll find a way to talk privately. Promise me that, okay, honey?"

Melissa promised her mom that she would keep talking with her whenever she felt that things were getting too much for her to handle. She also told her mom that Brad had confronted her that morning and forced the issue. He could tell that she was in love and unhappy about it because he had been in love himself in the past. So now both Kay and Brad knew. Melissa told her mom that she knew that they would both help her as much as they could, even while keeping her secret.

She mopped up her tears, and they went shopping for a little while. Kay bought Melissa a pretty new sweater that they both saw and immediately loved. Kay said that it was a little young for herself, but it would look lovely on Melissa. Melissa promised to wear it next week at the family dinner. They talked about the family for a while and headed home. By the time they got home, Melissa was in a cheerful frame of mind. She smiled and readily greeted her dad with a kiss when he asked her if they had a good time. She left their home, feeling blessed to have such wonderful parents. She loved them more now than she had ever done when she was growing up as a lonely teenager.

CHAPTER
NINE

The volunteers were nearly finished with the Shelter's second project house. One more Saturday, and it would be completed. That Saturday, Melissa and Brad arrived at the site, ready to show Erik and Greta that they were a couple. They looked around and saw the regular crew. Mark was giving Erik, Greta, and Tommy some directions. When he saw Melissa walking over with Brad, he asked Erik to wait. He decided that Greta and Melissa should partner up painting the bedroom walls. That left Brad to partner with Erik and Tommy. Melissa wanted to argue with Mark but worried that he would wonder why she didn't want to work with Greta. Melissa looked at Brad with a question in her eyes. Brad pursed his lips and shrugged. Before the groups took off to do their work, she went over to Brad and gave him a hug. She whispered in his ear to be careful about what he said to Erik while they worked. Brad whispered back that he would be careful. Melissa got her supplies and walked over to Greta and said she was ready to go.

Erik watched Melissa hug Brad and whisper in his ear. They looked very loving to his jealous eyes. He was a bit ticked off with Mark for rearranging the groups, although he had to agree that it made more sense to partner with Brad than with Greta. Greta did not know how to handle a hammer, whereas he supposed that Brad would know how to do it.

He walked over to Brad, and they got their supplies. They started working on putting in some cupboards in the kitchen. Erik was surprised to see that Brad was handy with the tools needed for the day's work. He did not want to get to know Brad better, but it felt weird to work without talking at all, so he asked Brad about his job and other general things.

He found out that Brad had lived next door to Melissa for more than four years. Brad told Erik stories he hoped would indicate just how close he and Melissa were. He also made a few humorous remarks about some of his experiences with his dental patients. All of it was news to Erik, who did not know that Brad was a dentist.

As the day progressed, Erik was very surprised to find that he didn't mind working with Brad. Brad was a decent man, in his opinion. That realization made it worse for Erik. He wanted to hate Brad, but he found that he genuinely liked and respected him.

Erik took Tommy under his wing and showed him how to use some of the equipment. He used the hand-over-hand technique to show Tommy how to use a hammer and the electric sander. Tommy looked up at Erik, his face filled with admiration.

Brad watched Erik with Tommy. He was impressed with Erik and his gentle treatment of, and patience with, the young boy. He felt a tug at his heart when he realized how much Tommy needed someone like Erik in his life. He found that he was starting to like Erik. He felt bad for Melly. It certainly seemed to him that Erik was invested in Greta's little boy. He didn't know how much of this revelation he wanted to tell her when they got home that evening.

Melissa found it difficult to converse naturally with Greta. She tried her best, but even to her own ears, she sounded stiff. Greta seemed to feel the same way. They worked in uneasy silence until lunch.

When Mark called a halt for lunch, Melissa immediately found Brad and linked her arm with his. They went together to get their food and sat far away from the rest of the groups. She wanted to ask Brad about his morning's work. Brad just told her that they had calmly worked together while Erik helped Tommy learn how to use the tools. He said that he and Erik talked briefly about dentistry. Melissa was glad that nothing earth-shattering had been said between Brad and Erik. She told him about the awkward silence between herself and Greta. At that point, he gave her a quick hug to show his support.

Erik watched them out of the corner of his eyes. He thought that Melissa and Brad hugged a lot today. Maybe their relationship was getting deeper. Brad had certainly talked lovingly about Melissa in his conversation with Erik. Meanwhile, Erik was glad that this project house would be done after today. He really did not want to see how close Melissa and Brad were getting every time he volunteered. He might have to find a new volunteer project and stop seeing the Hillman group so much. Of course, he could always call in and see Mark, Matt, or Paul in the evenings when they were at home.

That evening, Paul and Sarah invited all the volunteers to their home for supper. They planned to grill some meat and vegetables on their deck. It was a nice evening. Greta and Tommy wanted to go, so Erik took them to Paul's house. He watched Melissa and Brad play with Christopher. They seemed so comfortable at Paul and Sarah's house.

Sarah's pregnancy was quite advanced by now. Melissa, Tessa, and Susan did as much as they could to help Sarah with the food and with Christopher. Erik saw Brad smooth back Melissa's dark curls when she was playing a hot and sweaty game with young Chris. They laughed a lot, too. Erik felt his heart wrench when he saw them together. He wondered how long it would be before the two of them got engaged to be married.

He tried to stay outside with the other guys, just so he did not have to watch Melissa and Brad together. He knew it was time to leave when he saw Brad hug Melissa and drop a kiss onto her cheek. She looked up at Brad and smiled so warmly at him. They walked back into the house, arm in arm. Erik collected Greta and Tommy, and they made their farewells to the Thompsons.

Erik dropped Greta and Tommy off at their cramped little apartment in the older part of town. She asked him to come in for something to drink. He agreed to come inside because he wanted to talk with her, anyway. Once inside the kitchen, he looked around. Greta's apartment was so dreary and small. He knew that Tommy's deadbeat dad had not sent money for them in months. Greta was trying to raise Tommy with just her grocery store income. He knew that she didn't make much money.

He was doing okay financially. He didn't have a huge amount of money, but he had enough to live comfortably. He always felt bad when he met someone so nice and deserving who was forced to scrape for every penny. He resolved to take Greta and Tommy out whenever he could. He wanted to make their lives a little better.

Greta told him to sit down at the kitchen table. Because he was such a large man, it was a tight fit. While the three of them drank their cold beverages, Erik wondered exactly how he would tell Greta that he just wanted them to be friends and nothing more.

Greta watched Erik and knew exactly what he was thinking about. She said to Tommy, "Sweetie, I would like you to go and play in your bedroom for a little while. I want to talk privately with Erik."

Tommy looked at her and then at Erik and gave them both a tooth-gapped grin. He set his glass in the sink. As he turned away from the sink, Tommy clenched his right fist and, flexing his right arm, pointed to the small bulge with his left hand, proclaiming, "Look, Erik! I'm already building muscles—just like you!" Then he dashed to Erik and hugged him, saying, "Thanks for showing me how to swing the hammer just like you."

Their large guest, who could scarcely be knocked over by anyone or anything, found himself quietly gasping for breath as Tommy's head burrowed into his midsection during a fierce hug. Erik gently rubbed Tommy's head and said, "That's right, Tommy. You did man's work today. When you're done playing, be sure to wash up, brush your teeth, and say your prayers before bed, you hear?"

Tommy beamed at Erik, released his mighty grip only to apply another gentler hug on his mother.

"Good night, Mommy," Tommy murmured.

"Good night, Tommy," Greta said with a tender smile. "Remember," she added, "you can play with your things for another thirty minutes, but first wash up, like Erik said."

Once again, Tommy looked adoringly at Erik before nodding yes to his mom and heading for the bathroom to wash his face and brush his teeth. He would gladly do anything that Erik told him to do. He loved Erik and hoped that they would always be friends. In his small hopeful heart, he wished that Erik was his daddy. He could tell that Mommy liked Erik, too.

After Tommy was out of sight, Erik was about to speak when Greta interrupted. "Erik, I know what you're going to say. You're not in love with me and just want us to go out as friends, right?" she smiled as she said that.

Erik was a little surprised but happy that he did not have to hurt her when he told her that. "How did you know, Greta?" he asked her.

"I have eyes in my head. You're in love with Melissa. It's too bad that she and Brad are dating. I think that she would be perfect for you," she told him quietly.

Erik looked down at his hands. He had not wanted anyone to see how he felt about Melissa. He asked her, "Greta, how could you tell? I thought that I had been careful about not letting it show. Do you think anyone else knows?" *Oh, please God, don't let Melissa know*, he prayed.

Greta gently told him, "I watched you today. You couldn't stop looking at her. No, I don't think anyone else noticed. I'm sure that Melissa did not notice. She didn't look at you at all. She and Brad seemed pretty close today. I'm so sorry, Erik. That must hurt you to know that she loves Brad."

Erik nodded and said, "Greta, this does not change anything between us. I still want to hang around with you and Tommy. Will you still let me take you guys out? You deserve better than this." He swept his hand around to indicate her surroundings.

She agreed to continue to go out with him as friends. Tommy would be very happy because he worshipped Erik. They talked for a few more minutes before Erik took himself home.

* * *

There was a big party at the St. Mary's Shelter recreation hall the next Saturday evening in gratitude for the volunteers who helped to build the two homes. Mark invited everyone who had worked at least one day on the project to the party. Melissa pressed Brad into coming with her for moral support. When they arrived, they saw Erik standing by the soft drinks with his one arm around Greta and his other hand hanging on to Tommy's hand. Melissa wondered if they had gotten engaged or anything like that.

She stuck as close as she could to Brad all evening. She visited with her family and the other volunteers. When she and Brad, hand in hand, made the rounds, they stopped next to Greta and Tommy, who were sitting alone for a few minutes.

"Hi, Greta. Hi, Tommy. Are you having a good time tonight?" Melissa asked them in a bright and cheerful voice.

"Oh, yes, everyone is so nice. Tommy and I have enjoyed getting to know everyone else who volunteered. It's a good feeling, building a house for some homeless family, isn't it? When Erik first told me about the project house, I never would have guessed how amazing it would feel to be a part of something so worthwhile. I can never thank him enough for all of the friendships I have made." Greta said with a few tears starting to form in her eyes. Melissa felt a kinship with her. She felt the exact same way about volunteering.

She smiled sweetly at Greta and asked her, "Is Erik getting you guys something to eat and drink? If not, Brad and I would be glad to do it. Or we would be willing to sit with Tommy while you went to get some."

She looked quickly at Brad with her eyebrows raised. Brad smiled at her and said that he would be happy to go and get all of them something to eat and drink.

Greta said, "No, Erik said that he wanted to talk with Mark for a minute and that he would pick up the food and drinks on his way back around. He asked me to save him a seat. I'm sorry that there are not two extra seats here for you both. You could drag a few chairs over here if you'd like to sit down with us. You are more than welcome to." She smiled sweetly at Melissa.

Melissa did not want to sit with them, but she did want to say a quick hello to Erik. She returned Greta's smile, even while she shook her head no. "We promised that we would sit with Sarah and Paul and help her take care of Christopher. She's getting so big now and finds it difficult to have Chris on her lap. Between Brad and I, we can take care of Chris for her. Have a nice time. We hope to see you at the next event." She looked at Brad who made a similar type of remark to Greta. As they walked towards Sarah, they ran into Erik, who was trying to juggle three plates of food. He stopped for a minute to talk with them.

"Hi, Melissa. Hi, Brad. How are you guys doing tonight?" he asked them with a smile.

Melissa smiled cheerfully at him and replied, "We're really good. It looks like you have your hands full. Can we help you take this food over to Greta? We just talked with her, and she told us that you were getting the food for them."

"That would be a big help, Melissa. Thanks. Let's drop this food off and go back for the drinks," he told her.

The three of them walked back to where Greta and Tommy were waiting. They set the food down. Erik ruffled Tommy's hair and said, "Here you go, Sport. Did your mom sign you up for the Cub Scouts, yet? Call me and let me know when your first meeting is, and I will come with you, just so you know where to go and everything. Are you looking forward to it?" he asked the little boy.

Tommy enthusiastically hugged Erik and said that he couldn't wait to meet the other Cub Scouts. Melissa thought again that Erik, Tommy, and Greta looked just like a young family. She wondered how serious Erik was about Greta. Maybe they planned to get married soon. There was no reason to wait. *They both must be in their mid-thirties,* she thought. She smiled at Greta, again, and turned to leave, her hand on Brad's arm.

Erik said, "Let's go and get those soft drinks. Where are you two sitting? You're welcome to sit with us."

Melissa told Erik that they planned to sit with Sarah and help her with Christopher. She and Brad walked back to the drinks station talking in a very general way with Erik. She picked out a drink for herself, urged Brad to do the same, and turned to Erik.

"Bye, Erik. Have a good time tonight. See you at the store in two weeks," she said with a brittle smile.

She turned away and went to sit with Sarah, Chris, and Paul. Brad, who saw that Melissa was hurting, put his arm around her and stayed by her side for the rest of the evening. They played with Chris while they chatted with the rest of the family. They were some of the first to leave the gathering. Melissa looked around and waved goodbye to her friends as they left.

When they got back to her apartment, she hugged Brad and thanked him for hanging out with her and being her support all night. He saw that she was sad, but she didn't want him to stay and talk. He left her apartment and went to his own. Melissa just curled up on her bed and cried herself to sleep that night.

Erik had watched Melissa and Brad with Christopher that evening. They looked exactly like a young couple with a small boy. He never had any inkling that he looked that way, himself, when he sat with Greta and Tommy.

Greta looked at Erik with compassion in her eyes. She could see that he was hurting. She thanked him for the wonderful evening and told him that she would call him and let him know when Tommy's first Cub Scout meeting was scheduled.

Melissa decided that she would stop attending the basketball games for the next few Thursdays. She really did not want to see Erik and Greta together. Her brothers frowned and complained when she told them that she was too busy to come to the games. She did show up frequently at their parents' house on Sundays for their regular lunch or supper dates. She was as friendly as ever to them, but they could all see that she continued to lose weight. Her laughter was forced, and she often looked sad without realizing it. Meanwhile, her sisters-in-law told her brothers to stop fussing; Melissa would tell them what was wrong when she was ready to do so.

Erik came into the store for his next meeting with Melissa. He was not sure how to treat her. He shouldn't have worried. Melissa was brightly cheerful but was hiding behind a professional barrier. Even if he wanted to talk personally with her, he was not able to penetrate her reserved demeanor. He wanted to ask her why she stopped coming to the basketball games, but she never gave him the chance to say anything of a personal nature. She briskly gave him her order and then ushered him out the door. He was out of there in ten minutes.

* * *

It was now the middle of October. Erik went to the flea market again, hoping to run into Melissa. He didn't have that kind of luck. However, he was able to find a few more things for his kitchen and bedroom. His house was looking much better these days. He had hung the beautiful tapestry on the wall in his bedroom. He remembered how much Melissa loved it and wanted to buy it. He looked at it often, picturing her face when she saw it in his bedroom. *Yeah, right, as if that would ever happen,* he thought morosely. He really liked the tapestry, too. It was the focal point in the room. He bought a new bedspread, pillows, and a rug that complimented the tapestry.

One night, Erik decided to visit Mark and Susan after work. He hadn't seen baby Sarah for quite a while. With his mom's help, he bought young Sarah a sweet and soft baby doll. He thought that it would look cute in the doll carriage that Melissa had given them. He knocked on the door about seven-thirty. He figured that they had eaten supper by now. Mark came to the door and happily let Erik in. Erik showed him the doll that he brought for Sarah.

Susan came into the room and eyed it. "Thank you, Erik. It was so nice of you to bring it for Sarah. She will love it. It is so soft that she will be able to hug it and drool on it," she said with a droll smile.

Erik sat on the couch with Sarah in his arms. He was a little nervous because he had not held many babies as young as Sarah. She felt so sweet in his arms. He thought, with surprise, that he wanted to have his own baby to love. He had never really given children a thought before, but now he realized that he would love to have a baby with Melissa. Sarah had the same coloring as Melissa—the same as all the Hillmans. Although Susan had big brown eyes and brown hair, baby Sarah had inherited her father's black hair and blue eyes. Melissa had that same coloring, in a less vivid hue.

The three of them talked for a while about the Shelter. Mark told Erik about a few more volunteer projects that he was trying to set up. At some point, he brought up the Thursday night basketball games. It was always a bit more difficult playing outside when winter came, with all the snow. The group always got there early to shovel off the court so that the boys could still play the game. Mark mentioned casually that Melissa hadn't been there for a few weeks.

That was unusual because she had been showing up so regularly to sit with Susan, Tessa, and Sarah.

Erik guardedly asked, "Maybe she and Brad do something together on Thursdays. The last few times I have seen them, they looked really close. Do you think that they are on the verge of getting engaged?"

Susan and Mark looked at him in astonishment. "Engaged?!! What are you talking about, Erik? Brad is Melissa's best friend. They're not dating. Oh, I know that they do a lot of things together, but they're not in love or anything like that. What made you think that?" Mark asked him incredulously.

Erik felt his heart stop. *What?!! Melissa and Brad are not dating and are not in love?* All this time he had agonized about Melissa loving Brad. Now Mark nonchalantly tells him that Brad and she are just best friends? It was too good to be true.

He must have looked dazed, because Susan quickly asked him, "Erik, why did you think that Melissa and Brad were dating? Did someone tell you that?"

He continued to look dazed and said, "No, no one ever told me that. It's just that I have seen them together so often. They seem so close. I had absolutely no idea that they were not a couple."

Susan looked at Erik thoughtfully. Erik appeared shocked when he heard about Melissa and Brad. Now she thought that he seemed very happy at the news. *Is Erik interested in Melissa?* she wondered. She knew from talking with her mother-in-law that Melissa liked someone. She was keeping it a big secret, though. The only one who knew anything was Kay Hillman, and she had sworn to Melissa that she would not tell the others. She would wait for Melissa to do that when she was ready. *Very interesting,* thought Susan. She wanted to ask Erik a few more questions.

"How do you get along with Melissa, Erik? I know that you are the sales rep for her store. Do you see much of her?" she asked casually.

"I see Melissa once a month at the store. Of course, I used to see her at the basketball games and when we were all volunteering. I can't say that I have seen much of her lately, though. She has been hanging out with Brad the last two or three times I've seen her. That's why I thought that they were dating," he told her, trying not to give himself away. He certainly did not want Mark and Susan to start getting any ideas about him. He wanted to sit quietly and think about this wonderful and unexpected news.

He changed the subject and chatted with Mark and Susan for another fifteen minutes before he told them that he had to go. He dropped a soft kiss on baby Sarah's head and reluctantly handed her back to Susan. Sarah had such a wonderful baby smell and her small little body was so sweet. Just before turning to leave, he promised that he would try to be available for the upcoming volunteer projects.

He drove himself home in a stupor. His brain kept telling him over and over, *Melissa is not in love with Brad. They are just friends.* He was happier about that than he could imagine. His pleasant thoughts came to a sudden halt. If Brad was not the cause of Melissa's reserved behavior, what was? She was obviously avoiding him again. He thought that they were becoming friends, but something happened to make her hide behind an impenetrable wall suddenly.

He had absolutely no idea that she might think he was involved with Greta. Whenever he went over all his conversations with Melissa in his mind, he automatically passed over anything that had to do with Greta. He never told anyone that he was dating Greta. Why would anyone even suppose that to be true? He didn't think about the fact that he put a friendly arm around Greta's shoulders or spent a lot of time with Tommy. He would have been very shocked if someone asked him if he and Greta were a couple. Because he did not think of Greta as a potential spouse, he didn't think anyone else would think that, either.

Now he was resolved to get to the bottom of Melissa's avoidance of him. If only she hadn't pulled that cloak of professionalism around herself. He had not been able to get behind it to see the real Melissa. He would have to think about a way to ask her about Brad. More than that, he wanted to show her in some way that he cared about her. *Only how?* he wondered.

CHAPTER
TEN

One evening, Melissa planned to meet Tollie's owners, Thomas and Timothy, at a nice pasta restaurant a few miles from the store. The brothers wanted to discuss plans for the upcoming holidays. She arrived before them and sat at their table, idly looking around her. The first person she saw was Greta Brown. She was sitting at a table with a nice-looking man of about forty or so. Tommy was there, as well, along with a slightly older boy of about ten or eleven. Greta caught Melissa's eye and beckoned her over. Intrigued, Melissa walked over to her table.

"Hi, Greta. How are you? It looks like we both had the good idea to try out the pasta tonight," Melissa said to Greta in a friendly voice. She wondered who this man was.

"Hi, Melissa. Let me introduce you to Bob Nelson. He and I grew up in the same town. Bob is a good friend of my older brother, Shane. We haven't seen each other for a long time. We dated a bit when I was in college before I met my husband. We lost track of each other when I moved away. Bob married a girl that I used to know, but he's now a widower. He and his son, Jimmy, just moved to Litton. My brother told him that I lived here, too, so he looked me up. We had a wonderful time talking about old times." Greta smiled shyly at Bob as she said that.

Melissa was very glad to see how happy Greta looked, but she wondered about Erik. Was he okay, or did this new interest in Greta's life hurt him? She felt terrible for Erik. Melissa and Greta talked for a few more minutes until she saw the Olson brothers arrive at their table. She excused herself and went to say hello to her dinner dates. While she talked with them, she looked at Greta's table a few times. Bob was holding Greta's hand. They seemed very happy together.

Melissa had to keep her wits about her. The Olson brothers had all kinds of ideas about Thanksgiving and Christmas sales promotions. She promised herself that she would think more about the Greta and Bob situation when she got home. The Olson brothers were quite happy with Melissa and the store's progress since she took over its management. Sales were significantly improved, and the brothers could finally see that they were not going to lose Tollie's. They hugged and kissed Melissa when they parted for the evening.

When Melissa arrived home later that night, she sat in her living room thinking about Erik and Greta. It appeared that Greta had found someone else. *What happened between Erik and her?* Melissa wondered. Of course, she had not seen Erik for weeks. Anything could have happened. Maybe he had broken up with Greta. Or had Greta broken his heart?

She sat in her pretty flowered chair, contemplating the whole situation and feeling sorry for Erik. How she hoped that he was not hurting as a result of Greta's new relationship with Bob. She wondered how she could discover what really happened. She knew that she could not just come out and ask Erik about it. They only had a professional relationship these days. *I'll just have to wait and see,* she concluded.

Sarah's second baby was due any day now. Her baby shower was one to which the men were invited, as well as her female friends and relatives. Paul and Sarah already knew that they were having another baby boy. They planned to name him Mark, in honor of Paul's lifelong friendship with Mark Hillman. They confided to their closest friends that it seemed as if their dreams were coming true. Before they married, both Sarah and Paul had a dream that they would have two sons and then a daughter.

The shower was held at the recreation center of St. Mary's Shelter because the Thompson's living room couldn't comfortably entertain the number of invited guests. Melissa agreed to bring her famous brownies to the shower. The other invitees also contributed food and drinks so that Sarah and Paul could just relax instead of having to prepare all the refreshments for such a large crowd. Paul's mother, Vivian, was the hostess for the event. Paul's sister, Kelly, assisted her mother with everything since their mom's health was currently a little shaky.

Melissa got to the baby shower early to help set up the food and drinks. Helping hands had decorated the center with lots of light and dark blue balloons and streamers. It looked quite festive. Young Christopher was tickled pink as he stared in awe at the balloons. Melissa watched over him and laughed at his antics as he tried to release as many balloons as he could reach.

There were thirty or more guests at the shower. Brad and Melissa arrived together. He was quite friendly with Sarah and Paul. Melissa thankfully put a squirming Christopher in Brad's arms while she helped arrange the food on the banquet tables. Brad took Chris into the corner that was set up for the little ones. Here the floor was carpeted, and there was an ample supply of toys to keep them entertained. He sat down with Chris and got him involved in playing with the toy trucks.

Melissa caught a glimpse of Erik arriving with Greta and Tommy. They looked happy to be together, but Melissa couldn't help but notice that Erik did not hold her hand or have his arm around her. They just looked like good friends. Melissa was happy to see that. She was worried that Erik may have had his heart broken when Greta started to go out with that Bob. She had been worried ever since meeting Bob that night at the pasta restaurant. However, Erik did not look broken-hearted in the least. In fact, she could see that he had a huge smile on his face. She wondered about that. *What is up with Erik?* she wondered.

Melissa watched him go up to the food table and snag a few brownies. He grinned widely and walked up to her. "Yum," he groaned with pleasure and an eye roll for good measure—all for the benefit of the baker who created these masterpieces. Melissa grinned and blushed a little.

Erik swallowed his brownie and said, "I had hoped that these bad boys would be here tonight." He offered her one of them. She took it and smiled nicely at him. She leaned in close to him and said in a conspirator's whisper, "I made an extra batch for you. They are in my car. Make sure that you grab them before you leave tonight." She stood in front of him with bright eyes and a happy smile.

Erik looked at her and thought that she was exquisite. He gave her a quick loose hug and said, "That is the best news that I have heard in a long time. Thank you so much, Melissa. Now I won't have to steal a bunch of them to take home with me."

Kelly and Vivian called out for everyone's attention. The shower was about to begin. Sarah and Paul were sitting in comfortable chairs in the front of the recreation center. There was a microphone nearby so that everyone would be able to hear whatever was said. A huge pile of gifts resided on a large table next to Paul. Tessa sat next to him with their Baby Book. She was going to record each gift and its donor in it so that Sarah and Paul would have a record of the day. Melissa and Brad had seats at the table directly in front of them. Chris was tired and taking a quick nap on Brad's lap.

Melissa watched as Paul and Sarah opened the gifts and exclaimed over them. Because this was their second boy, they already had quite a few of the necessary baby things, so they received many more pieces of clothing and personal items for the newborn instead. Melissa thought that the tiny boy's clothes were just adorable. Little boys' clothing had certainly become more fashionable. No longer was everything just red or blue. Melissa watched happily as Paul opened her gift to them. It was a beautiful china figure of two little boys playing together. The word "Brothers" was printed across the bottom. Their two sons were going to share a large bedroom. She knew that Paul and Sarah had a nice shelf in the boys' room that they hoped to fill with figurines and inspirational words. This would be the first of many china figures, she was sure. Sarah and Paul held up the figure and looked at Melissa with friendship and love. They told her that they loved it and would put it on the shelf right away. They opened Brad's gift next. It was an unimaginative little boy's outfit in blue. They thanked Brad very nicely. Melissa dug her elbow into Brad's side and teased him about his predictable gift. He just smiled at her and shrugged.

The gift opening took nearly an hour. When the gifts had all been opened and recorded, they were set on the waiting table for everyone to look at over the lunch break. Lots of people surged forward to the banquet table for their food and drinks. Melissa and Brad were close to the table and were among the first ten or so to go through the line. They filled their plates and went back to their seats to eat. They took young Chris with them.

Melissa helped Chris eat his food. She looked around at the crowd of people. She knew almost everyone there. People stopped by to talk with her and Brad. She was having an enjoyable time. A little later, Greta and Tommy paused at Melissa's table on their way to get their food. Greta shyly walked up to Melissa and smiled at her. She discreetly showed Melissa the new engagement ring on her finger.

Eyes sparkling brightly, she told Melissa, "Bob proposed to me last night. We are going to get married next month. We have so many things in common. There is really no need for us to wait. Tommy and Jimmy get along so well together, too. Tommy loves having an older brother to teach him things and to hang out with. I hope that you and Brad will come to our wedding. We asked Mark if we could have the reception here in the rec center. If I send you an invitation, do you think that you will be able to come to the wedding?"

Brad looked very surprised. He had not known about Greta and Bob. Melissa forgot to tell him about seeing them together at the pasta place. Now Melly could find out if Erik had any feelings for her. He was so very pleased and excited for Melly. She deserved all the happiness she could get. He turned to Greta, extended his sincerest regards, and promised that he would come if he was available. He looked at Melissa with a question in his eyes. She smiled ecstatically at him and nodded.

She told Greta to drop the invitation off at the rec center, and she would get it from Mark. Melissa watched them walk away. She, in turn, was watched closely by Erik and her mother. Both could see that she looked very happy. Kay Hillman thought she knew the reason for Melissa's happiness, but Erik wondered about it.

He closely watched Melissa's behavior with Brad tonight. They acted like good friends but certainly not like two people who were in love. He wondered why Greta's engagement should make Melissa so overtly happy. He didn't think that she and Greta were such great friends. *It must be some other reason,* he thought. He hoped that he would have a chance to talk with Melissa without Brad hanging around. He wondered if he dared to stop by her apartment one evening, but what reason could he give her for doing that?

The shower lasted for about two hours. Melissa had a wonderful time conversing with her friends. Her secret happiness about Greta's engagement caused her to bubble over with joy. It had been a long time since her family and friends had seen her this visibly happy—which, of course, caused some to wonder, but the shower was no place to talk seriously about anything. It remained that only Brad and Kay knew her secret. Still, Mark and Matt and their wives intended to find out what was going on with their little Melly—maybe at the next family lunch on Sunday.

Erik asked Greta and Tommy if they could wait for a ride home. He wanted the chance to go with Melissa to her car and pick up the brownies that she made for him. They happily agreed to wait for him. They all helped with the clean-up. He carried presents and leftover food to various cars. At last, most of the other guests had gone. Only family was left.

Erik walked over to where Brad and Melissa were talking with Sarah. Their hands were filled with leftover food. Sarah hugged them and then turned around to look for Paul. He held Chris in one arm and put his other arm protectively around his wife. He carefully guided his family out to their car. Together, Melissa and Brad turned to look at Erik. Brad grinned widely at Erik and stuck out his hand in a gesture of friendship.

Erik was surprised but grinned back at him and shook his hand. He turned to Melissa and said, "Okay, Melissa, I am ready to take possession of those brownies." Anyone overhearing Erik's request and seeing the broad smile on his face could easily presume that the source of his happiness was the thought of receiving Melissa's delicious creations.

"I promise to share some with my mom. She and I are having lunch together tomorrow," Erik explained. He caught her eye as he continued, "If you ever decide to stop managing Tollie's, you could probably make a living selling these brownies. They are so tasty!" Then, turning to Brad, he warmly asked, "Brad, have you tried Melissa's secret recipe famous caramel nut brownies? They are the absolute best!"

Brad smiled and said, "Oh, yes, I have tasted those sinfully delectable brownies many times. I have even tried to be in her apartment when she makes them, but she always sends me home, so I can't find out her secret ingredients. It is a mystery, that's for sure. Did she make you a batch, Erik? If she did, she must prize your friendship greatly. I only ever get a few brownies at a time." With that, he gave a fake pout. Melissa was amused as she watched this exchange between the two men.

She laughed and batted Brad on the shoulder, saying, "Poor baby—don't lie. I have made batches for you to take to your office and to eat at your parties for several years." She turned to Erik and said, "It's true, though; I never let him watch me make them. I swear that I will go to my grave with the recipe intact."

They walked to her car. She got the container of brownies out of her trunk. She handed them over to Erik with a big smile. He took them, reached over, and kissed her cheek. Melissa blushed charmingly and said in a flustered voice, "You can keep the container. Use it for leftovers or something. I don't need it back."

Erik nodded and said, "Thanks so much. It was great of you to make these for me. I owe you one, now." His eyes twinkled when he secretly considered the ways that he could repay her. He didn't say anything more but waved his hand at them, collected Greta and Tommy, and went to his car.

Brad accompanied Melissa to her apartment. He helped her put away some of the leftover food. He agreed to come over in an hour or two for supper and help her eat up the leftovers. Before leaving, he hugged her and said, "Well, Melly, it looks like Greta is now out of the picture. I think that you should find out how Erik feels about you. From what I saw today, he is not unaware of you. He seemed quite friendly towards you. Do you want any help finding out? I can ask around, you know."

Melissa couldn't stop the happy smile from washing over her face. "No, Brad, I think that I can take it from here. I'm not sure how I'm going to discover his feelings for me, but I'll keep thinking about it. I don't have to do anything right away. Maybe I should just give it time and see what happens. We still run into each other at the basketball games and sometimes at family parties." She saw him out of the door and sat on her couch cuddling Clarabelle and thinking of exciting possibilities.

* * *

A week later, Sarah's new baby boy arrived. Paul shared the news with all their friends. By the time he finished making all the phone calls, he was flushed, and his ear felt like it would be numb for a week. Matt and Tessa took Christopher overnight when Sarah went into labor and for the next two days, as well. When Sarah and baby Mark came home from the hospital, they hosted a family get-together. Melissa wasn't quite family, but she was an "adopted sister" to them. She watched Paul as he walked around with the baby in his arms. He was so very happy with his young family. He filled the house with all of Sarah's favorite flowers just because she loved them, and he loved her more than life itself.

As Melissa witnessed their tender love for each other, she longed for that same kind of happiness for Erik and herself. She wondered if they would ever be more than friends. She knew that he was pleased with her gift of brownies, and he told her that he owed her something.

Yet she had no idea how to make him fall in love with her. It was a new idea for her. She would have to bide her time and see if anything developed between them. She was reassured by the thought that they would meet every month at the store. *But how can I make that meeting into something unforgettable?* she wondered.

Now that Brad was no longer an issue, Erik wondered how he could get closer to Melissa. Receiving a batch of her heavenly brownies was special in and of itself, but he wondered if maybe it meant something more. Meanwhile, he told her that he owed her something. What should he bring her? He didn't want to come on too strong and frighten her. He also did not want to give her time to fall in love with someone else. He had to proceed carefully. *If only Fate would intervene and help me out,* he thought.

CHAPTER
ELEVEN

It was a snowy day in early December. Melissa was at the store as usual. She and a few of the cashiers had just decorated the store with twinkle lights and a huge Christmas tree. She had the bright idea of tying small brightly wrapped gifts onto the tree. For every patron who spent thirty dollars in one transaction, they could choose a gift from the tree and take it home. She and her Christmas helpers made a list of small gifts that the patrons would enjoy. There were $5.00 gift cards for the store, candles, gum, candy, and plush animals. Every single gift came from Tollie's, so, while the store was being generous, they were also combining this act of kindness with shrewd marketing and smart inventory management. Melissa grinned as she contemplated the Olson's appreciation for her idea.

And, indeed, the Olson brothers thought that it was a marvelous idea. Once the patrons knew about the giveaway, they came in multiple times to partake in the promotion. One family already received four gifts from the tree. Each of the children in the family picked out their own gift.

Melissa made a point of being there to cheer on the gift recipients each time they qualified. A special bell was rung by the cashiers when someone earned the gift. Melissa enjoyed the happy customers and pleased cashiers. The cheery sound of a bell ringing added further joy to the season. Every night, she and her helpers filled the tree with more gifts. One day the store was so busy that they gave away twenty-five of the promotional gifts. Melissa was very pleased with the way things were going.

With the increased sales due to the promotion, the store soon depleted much of its inventory. Melissa quickly sent an email to Erik to place an additional order for December. He emailed back and said that he would come in the next day. The product shipment would come into the store a few days later.

Erik walked into the festive store and looked around with a big smile plastered on his face. It certainly looked as if Melissa had made the store profitable. Everywhere he looked, the store was busy, and patrons and employees alike seemed in a joyful mood. Christmas music was softly playing over the intercom.

Erik had stopped off at the mall before he arrived at Tollie's. He picked out a pretty, curly-haired angel ornament for Melissa. He put it in a festive Christmas gift bag. It was a thank you gift for the brownies. He peeked around the corner of her office and saw her bent over some papers.

"Hi, can I come in?" he asked her in a friendly voice.

"Erik, please come in," Melissa said, smiling sweetly at him.

His heart beat faster as he gazed upon her beaming face. He came into her tiny office and set the small gift bag on her desk and grinned at her.

"What's this?" she asked inquisitively. She looked up at him. His dark blond hair was full of snowflakes because it was snowing heavily outside. He shook his head like a big shaggy dog to rid himself of the snowflakes, and they dropped all over her floor.

Shaking his head one last time, Erik said ruefully, "I'm sorry. I should have brushed the snow off before coming into your office." With eyes drawn to the evidence already melting at his feet, he answered her question, "This is just a small thank you for the brownies. I saw this, and it reminded me of you. I hope you have a Christmas tree on which you can place this."

Melissa opened the bag and took out the ornament. She held it carefully in both of her hands. She first examined it and then looked up at Erik, who was still standing in front of her desk. She got to her feet and came around to the front of the desk where he was standing.

She smiled a very sweet smile and said, "You probably didn't know that I collect angels, but I have done so for many years. I don't have this one. She's beautiful. Thank you, Erik. I will gladly put her on my tree this year. Even though I have already decorated my tree, there is still plenty of room for her."

Her eyes were sparkling with happiness; she reached up and kissed Erik's cheek. His arms came around her, and he gave her a gentle hug. He released the embrace quickly, and they smiled into each other's eyes for a moment.

"You are so welcome, Melissa. I wanted to tell you that my mom loved your brownies, too. She said they were the best she had ever tasted." His voice was soft and sincere.

Melissa wanted to stay professional while they talked about her new order for the store. After ten minutes, they were finished. They then talked comfortably for a few more minutes about the Shelter. The promotional bell rang, signaling another customer's attainment of a gift. Melissa led Erik out of her office in time to see the customer choose a gift from the tree. He stood next to her and listened to her explain the promotion. *It is a genius idea,* he thought.

They talked for a few more minutes and then Melissa regretfully said that she had to end their chat because she needed to meet with someone. Erik said goodbye, but he told her to email again if she needed any more groceries. His regular meeting date was the 28th of the month, so he said he would see her then. As he walked out of the store, he wondered if he could see her before Christmas. He was glad that he had at least given her the angel.

* * *

Erik decided to have a Christmas party at his newly decorated home. He had not hosted a party for quite a few years. He asked his mom to help him with the invitations. He requested that the invitees bring a gift suitable for a youth or adult at St. Mary's Shelter. The people who sheltered there would need some more supplies. He especially wanted to make sure that the children had gifts to open.

He promised to have a gift-wrapping station set up in one of the rooms in his house so that people could bring the gift, show it to the others, and then wrap it up nicely. His mom promised to help him purchase all the necessary items for professional gift-wrapping. He knew that opening a pretty package was part of the fun of receiving a gift.

As he prepared for the party, he got more excited about it all the time. He invited the volunteers from the Shelter, as well as Greta, Tommy, Bob, and Jimmy. He also invited Paul and Sarah, Mark and Susan, Matt and Tessa, and Melissa and Brad. He was looking forward to seeing all of them again, especially Melissa. He had even gleefully hung up some mistletoe in a few secret spots. Of course, there was only one certain someone he hoped to catch under it.

The party was set for December 20th. Nearly everyone he invited accepted his invitation. Since he was not a great cook, he arranged to have the food catered. He set up the drinks station himself. His mom arrived early and helped the caterers set up the food in the kitchen.

The guests began arriving at 7:00 pm. His master bedroom held their coats. Meanwhile, his spare bedroom held the gift-wrapping station. He closed his office door. *There is no reason for anyone to go in here,* he decided.

The kitchen smelled wonderful with all the festive food. *The living room looks great,* he thought. His mom, Greta, and Tommy had come over a few days ago and helped him decorate a huge Christmas tree. Although it took up quite a bit of the wall in his living room, Erik thought it set the proper theme for the season.

His guests walked around, investigating the rooms in his house. None of them, except Greta, Tommy, and his mom, had ever been to his house before. Melissa arrived alone with a bag full of gifts. She told Erik that Brad was unable to make it to the party.

He took her coat and walked it into his bedroom. She was curious, so she followed him. She immediately saw the beautiful tapestry gracing one of the walls in his bedroom. He hadn't sent the promised text regarding the tapestry, so she did not know what had happened to it. It looked nice on the wall. Erik had color-coordinated his bedspread, pillows, and rug to match it. She stood there, admiring the tapestry.

Erik turned and saw her standing behind him. Just at that moment, he realized that he had not taken a picture of it and texted it to her. "I'm sorry, Melissa. I forgot to text you the picture of the tapestry when I put it up. It looks good there, doesn't it?" he asked hopefully.

Melissa nodded and shyly replied, "I wondered what your house looked like now after you finally decorated it. You have done a great job with these rooms. I guess you are a good student." She winked as she said this and noted a slight blush on Erik's face. "You certainly made this house into a very comfortable place."

She admired the several pieces of china and resin animals that he had on his dressing room table. She saw the chickadees right away. She stooped low to examine them, again. She was glad that he bought them. They looked cute along with the other figures of animals that were grouped together on his dresser.

Erik took her on a tour of the whole house. She especially liked his kitchen, which he had decorated in cobalt blue and white, with touches of golden yellow. She thought that it looked like it had a woman's touch. He saw her face and read her thoughts exactly.

"My mom helped me decorate the kitchen. We had a great time at that big discount home store looking at all the choices. I like the combination of blue and gold, and we found so many things in those colors. I guess other people like that combination, too. It was actually kind of fun decorating the house when I had someone who was willing to come with me and give their opinion," he told her.

Erik put on some Christmas music, and everyone circulated around the house. Some took up positions in the kitchen; others sat in the living room. Melissa brought a number of gifts with her for the kids at the Shelter, so she spent a good amount of time in the spare bedroom wrapping them. While she worked, she had a nice talk with Alison, who was supervising the room.

Alison, who knew all about Melissa and the fact that Erik was in love with her, casually asked Melissa some questions. She knew, more than ever, that Melissa was the right girl for her son.

Melissa finished wrapping her gifts for the Shelter kids. She then took two brightly wrapped gifts out of her large bag and secretly put them under Erik's tree. She placed the Christmas cards that she brought for Alison and Erik in a basket that was on the kitchen table.

Because she always thought of Erik as a Viking, she had found a very nice picture of the Minnesota Vikings football team and wrapped it up for Erik. She couldn't believe it when she came upon a sweet ornament of a blond nurse while shopping for Alison's Christmas gift. They were not expensive gifts, and she hoped that neither of them would feel weird that she had given them each something for Christmas.

Melissa knew all the guests at the party and enjoyed talking with them. By the end of the evening, there was a huge pile of gifts, fifty or more, to take to the Shelter. Since Mark went there every day, he volunteered to take them with him. He and Susan now had a minivan, so they had enough room in it for all the gifts.

Erik made a short speech to his guests about how appreciative he was for all their generous gifts to the people at the Shelter. A few of the volunteers who had families left the party early. By ten o'clock, only the Hillman brothers and their wives, Melissa, and the Thompsons were still there. Alison had told Erik that she would stay the night and help him with the clean-up when everyone left.

They all sat comfortably in the living room and talked generally about the Shelter as well as their plans for Christmas. Earlier, Matt had discovered the mistletoe in the living room and kitchen and took advantage of every opportunity to kiss Tessa under them whenever she walked by. Everyone good-naturedly teased him about his quest for kisses. He wiggled his eyebrows in a sultry way as he grabbed Susan, Sarah, and Alison when they happened to walk under the mistletoe. He gave them each a big smacking kiss on the lips.

There was a bunch of laughter about that. Tongue in cheek, he apologized to Melissa for not kissing her, but after all, she was his sister. Paul laughingly pulled Melissa under the mistletoe and planted a kiss on her, declaring that Melissa was not HIS sister. Melissa laughed so hard that tears rolled down her cheeks. She smilingly wiped them away and sat back down.

Erik looked at her surreptitiously. *Here is my chance to kiss Melissa,* he thought. Mark and Paul made the excuse to kiss their wives under the mistletoe, as well. The next time Melissa went into the kitchen to get a soft drink, Erik followed her. He stood under the mistletoe and waited for her to come back through. The others saw what he was about to do and hooted in laughter, teasing him. He looked at them with a wicked grin and put his finger to his lips to shush them.

When Melissa came back into the living room, she inadvertently walked under one of the sprigs. Erik caught her up into his arms and planted a big smacking kiss on her lips. She was shocked and blushed a deep red. He quickly pressed another, softer kiss, on her mouth before he let her go. They had to endure a lot of teasing for those kisses. Erik just smiled widely and shrugged, as if to say, "What about it?"

Melissa sat down and parried the comments from her brothers. She said, "Well, it's just that I am so darn kissable. You can't blame the guys. They can't help themselves." That shut her brothers up a bit. Paul and Erik, being the two men who had kissed her, just grinned and nodded.

Erik personally thought, *you're right, Melissa, I couldn't help myself*. In his mind, the whole party had been worth it for those two quick kisses on Melissa. Now that he had a taste of her, he wanted to give her a genuine kiss, filled with the passion he felt for her. He couldn't think how he would be able to do that, but he could fantasize about it when everyone had gone home.

Alison looked at Melissa with a thoughtful smile. Erik had put himself back out there when he kissed Melissa. He had not been that light-hearted in years. He had always been so intense and serious when he was with Diane. He was a friendly man, but not given to frivolous actions. She totally approved of his actions of kissing under the mistletoe. In fact, she was surprised that he had put the mistletoe up in the first place. At least, she suspected that he was the one who had placed it up there. Maybe it was one of the other guys. *But when could they have done it?* she wondered. *No, it was probably Erik,* she thought, smiling inwardly.

It was getting late and everyone started to go home. Melissa walked to the bedroom to get her coat. She looked around Erik's bedroom one last time. She totally approved of what she saw. *Erik made it into a comfortable haven,* she thought.

As Erik stood at his front door and said good night to his guests, he kissed the cheeks of the women as they exited. When he kissed Melissa goodnight, he held her hand for a few delicious seconds before smiling at her. His good night echoed in her ears as she drove home. *It was certainly a night to remember,* Melissa thought.

Erik and Alison quickly cleaned up the mess and then went into the living room to sit down and relax. He casually looked around the room and to his surprise, he saw the two gifts that were under the tree. He had not yet put any gifts under there, so they kind of stuck out. He pulled them out from under the tree. He looked at the gift tags and was surprised and very pleased to see that they were from Melissa.

He brought his mom's gift over to her and said, "Mom, this gift is for you from Melissa. I have one here, too. Why do you think she gave us a gift?"

Alison had already told him months ago that she had met Melissa at the store and had given her more sunburn lotion. She had admitted that they had talked for an hour. Erik was really surprised that his mom had done that. When he had questioned her more closely about it, she had shrugged and said that she just wanted to be helpful to Melissa since she had been so helpful to Erik at the flea market. Erik had to admit that it did sound like something his mom would do.

Alison looked at her nicely wrapped gift and smiled. "Melissa seems the type of woman to give gifts to all of her friends. Did you see the gifts she brought to wrap tonight? I helped her wrap them. She had seven gifts for the kids at the Shelter. She seems to be a very generous woman. I wonder what she gave us. Do you want to unwrap it early so you can find out? That way you can decide if you want to get her anything in return." She looked at Erik with a question in her eyes.

Erik raised his eyebrows and nodded. He wanted to get her a gift but wondered if it would be inappropriate. But now that she had given him something, he could think about giving her something in return. He wasn't sure what he could give her, but he would go shopping and look around. Because he had been to her apartment, he knew the kinds of things that she treasured. "Let's open them, Mom. You go first," he told her.

Alison opened the gift and looked at the sweet little nurse ornament. She smiled at the whimsy of it. Although she had been a nurse for thirty-plus years, no one had ever given her a nurse ornament before. She asked Erik if she could put it on his tree. She only had a miniature Christmas tree in her apartment and this ornament would be the wrong size for her little tree.

He agreed, and she carefully put it on a branch at eye level. Whenever she looked at the tree, she would be reminded of Melissa. She thought that Erik would also think of her when he saw it.

Erik's gift was much larger than Alison's. He slowly opened the gift. When he saw the picture, he laughed. His friends had been giving him Vikings things for years. He did like the Minnesota Vikings football team, but that was not why his friends gave him Viking-themed items. It was because of his ethnic background and the fact that he honestly looked like a Viking from long ago.

Erik wondered if it was just a coincidence or if Melissa thought that he looked like a Viking, as well. He looked it over carefully. It was a nice gift, and he would hang it on one of his walls. He gave it to his mom, so she could look at it. She privately thought that it was a nice safe gift, not too personal, but something that most men might enjoy. *Melissa is playing it safe,* she thought with a small grin.

CHAPTER
TWELVE

Erik took his mom shopping the next day. He found a very sweet china figurine of a cat that looked exactly like Clarabelle. Melissa told him last night that she collected china animals and had some in her bedroom. Alison found a ceramic puppy that looked like a young Rusty that she wanted to give to Erik at first. But he was with her when she found it, and he had seen it. It wouldn't be much of a surprise if she were to give it to him.

He thought that Melissa might like it. She told him that she loved dogs. It was too bad that he had to take Rusty to the vet before his party. Rusty had to stay there a few days. Erik would have enjoyed introducing Melissa to Rusty at the party.

They took their gifts back to his house and wrapped them prettily. There was still quite a bit of the wrapping paper, bows, and string left from his party. He had to think about when he could get the gifts to Melissa. Perhaps he could drop by her apartment in the next few days before Christmas.

He decided to drop by Melissa's apartment the very next day. Of course, he could drop his gifts off at the store, but there would be no privacy there. He wanted the chance to sit in her living room with her and talk in comfort and privacy. *Maybe we could start to get to know each other better,* he contemplated hopefully.

The next evening, he made his visit when he thought that Melissa would be home. It was seven pm. He buzzed her apartment. When she asked who was there, he said cheerfully, "Hi, Melissa. It's Erik. I have a few things to drop off for you. May I come up for a minute?"

There was a pause for a moment until she said, "Of course, I'll buzz you in. Come on up."

She ran into her bedroom quickly and changed her sweater for a prettier one and sprayed a little perfume on herself. She was next to her front door when he knocked on it. She opened the door and let him in. She looked at the two gifts in his hand, shook her head, and smiled briefly. "Come in, Erik."

He came into her apartment and looked around. She had a large Christmas tree that was all lit up with blue twinkling lights. There were lots of pretty ornaments on the tree. He saw his gift of the pretty curly-haired angel right at eye level in the front. It was in an optimal spot. The lights on the tree were the only ones that were on in that room, so the backdrop of darkness enhanced the cheery mood set by the beautiful Christmas tree. Instrumental Christmas music was playing from her entertainment center. The room looked cozy and very comfortable.

She ushered him into the room and asked him to sit down on the couch. Clarabelle immediately jumped up on his lap. He grinned at the cat and said, "And how are you, Miss Clarabelle? I haven't seen you for a while. I hope you've been a good kitty for your mommy."

Melissa grinned at this gentle side of Erik that she found so attractive. "Oh, she has been a good kitty. I think that Santa will have a few presents for her this Christmas."

Erik handed her the two gifts. "Mom and I wanted to thank you for the gifts you left us," he said cheerfully.

"You opened them already, didn't you?" she asked him in an amused but accusing voice.

He had the decency to look suitably chastised and said, "Well, I never could resist an early gift. My mom could never put my gifts out early for fear that I would shake them to death or unwrap them and then re-wrap them before Christmas." He looked like a naughty little boy when he confessed this to her.

She bubbled up with laughter and said, "Okay, now I know. Don't expect to get any more gifts early from me. If I give you a gift, it will be right on time and not early. I see that you can't be trusted," she laughed a little in good humor.

He looked at her seriously for a second and said, "Thank you for the Vikings picture. I'll find a place to hang it on one of my walls. And Mom loves the nurse ornament. In all these years, she has never gotten a nurse ornament. It was very nice of you to give us each a gift. It was totally unexpected, but nice."

Melissa looked down at her hands and said quietly, "I wanted to give you each a small gift. I enjoy giving gifts to people I like." With that, she blushed bright red. He saw her blush but did not comment on it.

"Well, thank you, Melissa. You are a really nice person," he said graciously to her.

They talked for a few minutes about the store and the big sales that they were experiencing. Melissa offered him a soft drink, which he accepted. He wanted to stay a bit longer in her apartment. He stroked Clarabelle's fur while they talked. She purred loudly.

Erik found his courage and quietly asked her, "Melissa, would you go out for a meal with me sometime?" He looked at her intently as he asked, with a hopeful look on his face.

She looked at her hands for a second or two and then looked him straight in the eyes. "Yes, Erik, I would like to go out with you. When and where do you want to go?" she asked softly.

Erik felt relieved. Taking a breath, he replied, "Do you have any time before Christmas? I know it's only a couple of days away. Or would it be better to wait until after Christmas? You can choose, Melissa," he smiled at her.

She thought about it and said, "Well, we're probably both quite busy before Christmas. I know that the week after Christmas is not as busy for me. How about the 28th? You are supposed to come to the store that day for my order. Why don't we think about where we want to go and talk about it when you come into the store on the 28th? If you are not busy that night, we can go somewhere after we get off work. How does that sound?"

He nodded his approval, saying, "That's perfect."

They talked and relaxed, listening to the music, for another half an hour. Erik reluctantly got up to go. He put Clarabelle gently on the floor. As he walked to the door, Melissa walked beside him. He turned to her and put his arms around her. He bent and kissed her very sweetly on her mouth. She kissed him back, just as sweetly. Erik felt a shot of joy rush through him. Melissa obviously liked him a bit. She kissed him back. *That is a very good sign,* he thought.

After he left, Melissa thought a lot about Erik and his kiss. She had been unable to stop herself from kissing him back. She wanted him to continue kissing her. She loved the feel of his strong arms around her. She knew by now that he was a gentle person. So many large men were, it seemed. She thought tenderly that Erik would make a wonderful husband and father. Even if he sometimes became impatient, she thought that he would always put his wife and children first. She thought he would be the type of man to cherish his wife and children. She had never felt cherished in her life, but she longed for Erik to cherish her.

She was ecstatic that he asked her for a date. Asking Erik out was a possibility, but that was not her style. She did not chase after men. Melissa decided that she would keep their upcoming date a secret from Brad and her mom. They were the only people who knew about her love for Erik. After their date, she would know what to tell them.

On Christmas Eve, Melissa received a Christmas card in the mail from Erik and Alison. It was a cute little dog howling to the chorus of Jingle Bells. She loved it. She had opened her gifts from Erik and Alison that morning. *Well, I waited until Christmas*, she told herself. It *was* Christmas Eve. She held the dog and cat figurines and showed them to Clarabelle. She found a spot on her shelves in her bedroom for the them both.

She dressed up to go to her parents' house. According to Hillman Christmas tradition, they opened two gifts on Christmas Eve and then later went to midnight mass. Her mom always prepared a special supper, and they all sat around talking and playing games. They liked card games and cribbage. Her dad used to bring home a different board game every Christmas. They would learn how to play it and then played the heck out of it during Christmas and the month after. By February, the whole family was tired of the game, and they would put it away or give it to Goodwill. Then they would do it all again with a different board game the next Christmas. Nowadays, they just played cards and cribbage.

Baby Sarah had at least a dozen gifts under the tree. Melissa looked at them and laughed. Sarah was too young to even appreciate any of them this year. She thought about next year's Christmas. Matt and Tessa would have their baby by then, and Sarah would be one and a half years old. Christmas would be so much fun with the little ones.

For the first time in her life, Melissa started to seriously daydream about getting married and having her own babies. Maybe she and Erik would get married next year. She was absolutely thrilled at that thought. Apparently, she was so overjoyed in her musings that her face gave her away.

Her mom looked at her with raised eyebrows. *Oh no, I wasn't going to say anything to Mom about my upcoming date with Erik. I might have blown it. Mom could always get information out of us kids. She is a master of the inquisition,* Melissa thought ruefully.

Thankfully, the moment passed without Kay asking a single question. Still, Melissa knew better than to think that Kay hadn't noticed something and subsequently stored the information for later use.

Melissa looked at Tessa. She was as big as a house. At seven and a half months pregnant, her belly was way out of proportion with her petite body. She waddled along, looking very uncomfortable. She preferred to wear Matt's flannel shirts instead of maternity clothes. When she was with family, she wore his shirts for comfort. She would only dress in her maternity clothes for special occasions. Because she was such a small woman, most of the maternity tops hung down and looked like dresses on her. "Someone should design maternity tops for petite women," Tessa always said. Susan had a similar problem. She was only five-foot-three inches tall. But she was still taller than Tessa's five-foot-one-inch body.

Recognizing that she was daydreaming, Melissa employed her workday focus mentality and forced herself back to the matters at hand. It was Christmas time at the "Hillman House", and she needed to be on her toes. A question about her personal life could come from her brothers or mom at any moment.

Melissa watched as Matt came over to Tessa and gently hugged her and kissed the top of her curly head. After a year of marriage, he was still amazed that this very wonderful tiny little dynamo loved him and had married him. Although she still possessed a fiercely independent nature, every cell in his body just wanted to protect her and keep her safe and happy. He could tell that she was uncomfortable with this pregnancy. He made her lie down every day and would rub her feet until they felt better.

Melissa watched him lovingly and tenderly stroke Tessa's hair and her extended stomach. Prior to his marriage to Tessa, Melissa never really thought of Matt as being a romantic man, but she saw, again, how very much he loved his wife.

He went through hell a year ago when he believed that Tessa would marry another man. It was after he was seriously hurt at his job that Tessa's true feelings for Matt became evident. Her actions showed the Hillman family that she loved him.

Matt wasted little time before claiming Tessa for himself. They married within two weeks and honeymooned for an additional two weeks in Paris, France. *Matt will be a great father,* Melissa thought.

Melissa had lots of time to observe Mark and Susan, too. Mark loved his baby, Sarah, so much. He proudly carried her everywhere. She often went to work with him for an hour or two so that Susan could have a break. Susan was the absolute love of Mark's life. He couldn't stop touching her and kissing her, even when there were other people around. He had some pretty deep emotions, and you could see and feel the chemistry between them. Susan was a happy and vivacious woman who adored Mark and his whole family.

Melissa felt as close to Susan as any biological sister. Melissa felt blessed to be a part of this very loving family. She wanted to tell them about Erik, but she also wanted to wait until there was something substantial to tell them. She knew that since they were each happily married, her brothers and their wives all hoped that Melissa would find her true love. Then all three Hillman siblings could live happily ever after.

Kay and Roy Hillman were still happily married after forty years of marriage. Kay was a vivacious and beautiful woman, and Roy was an attractive and wonderful man. He kept her from doing too much and getting too involved with everything. He was the yin to her yang. Melissa had watched their happy marriage her whole life and had sometimes felt a little left out. Her brothers were so much older than herself, and her parents had each other.

Now was Melissa's time for love. She truly hoped that she and Erik would find it together. She was sure about her feelings for him, but she had no idea about his feelings for her. December 28th could not come soon enough in her opinion.

Kay found time to get Melissa alone for a few minutes. "Melly, I've been watching you. You seem extraordinarily happy tonight. What has happened? Have you talked with Erik or something?" she quietly asked her daughter.

"Mom, I found out that Greta is getting married to an old flame from her college days. She and Erik were just friends—kind of like my friendship with Brad. He came over to my apartment a few days ago to drop off some gifts from his mom and him. I had given them both a small gift when I was at his Christmas party. Anyway, he asked me if I would go out for a meal with him. We are going out on December 28th. I'm not sure where, but we will talk about it when he comes into the store that day. I am excited about our date. Maybe I will find out that he likes me a lot. Oh, Mom, wouldn't it be wonderful if he loved me, too? Of course, it will only be our first date, so I can't expect anything from him right away. I can't stop smiling, though." Melissa's happiness was evident in her voice, and her eyes sparkled as she spoke.

Kay hugged Melissa and told her how happy she was for her. Because the other girls were walking closer to them now, they ended their discussion. Kay prayed that the date would go well for her Melly and that Erik would come forward with his love for her. After observing Erik that one night, Kay was convinced that Erik loved Melissa as much as she loved him.

Kay's life was so blessed right now. Her two sons were married to the loves of their lives, she had a granddaughter and another grandchild to be born in February, and now Melly might finally embark on the romance of her young life. Kay went over to her beloved Roy and gave him a big hug and a huge smile. He hugged her back and looked at her with total love in his eyes. He knew that she would tell him later what she was so happy about.

Erik and Alison had a quiet, but very nice, Christmas Eve and Day. Alison came over to his house and together they prepared the meals. It was nice just sitting and talking in the warm tree-lit living room, with soft music playing in the background. He told her about his upcoming date with Melissa. She saw and heard the deep contentment in his face and voice.

CHAPTER

THIRTEEN

On December 28th, Melissa was working at Tollie's. That afternoon she stopped what she was doing because she heard a commotion outside her office. One of the cashiers was running toward her. She stopped in front of Melissa and panted, "Ms. Hillman, the back storeroom is on fire! I went back there to get some more bread for the shelves, and when I opened the door, the flames shot out. I quickly closed the door and came to find you."

Melissa quickly told her, "Get all of the customers out of the store right now. I will call the fire department and the police. Please tell the other cashiers to evacuate with the customers. Only the members of the Safety Team should stay. Have them meet me right here, by my office. Go quickly, now." Melissa surprised herself a bit with her level of assuredness at this time, but now was not the time for reflection but rather action.

Melissa went into her office and called 911 to report the fire. After that, she called Thomas and Timothy Olson to tell them about the fire. That done, she waited outside her office for the three other members of her Safety Team. They got there quickly and looked to her for guidance. She was a little frightened, but she knew that the fire was currently contained in the back storeroom.

She and her team walked up and down each of the aisles in the store. They searched all bathrooms, other storerooms, and the break room in the store to make sure that every single person was out of the building. She hoped that the fire department would come quickly and be able to contain the fire to just the back storeroom. It would be a shame if the inventory and the store went up in flames, as well. When the team made sure that the building was empty save for themselves, she sent her team outside to sit in their cars. She had her walkie-talkie with her to recall them if she needed them. She stood in the entrance to the store to await the fire department and the Olson brothers.

When they arrived, she quickly took them to the back storeroom. They could see and smell the smoke by now. She assured them that the store was empty except for themselves. The firefighters were about to tell Melissa and the Olsons to leave the store when they all heard an explosion. The heavy door to the storeroom flew open and debris and sparks flew all around.

Melissa felt the sting of fire on her arms and the pain when some small piece of debris hit her forehead. The firefighters told them to go to the front of the store. They saw that Melissa and the Olson brothers had some cuts and small burns. They asked Melissa if she was okay and if she could call an ambulance. She nodded and guided the two older gentlemen to the front of the store. They were both shocked and had cuts and burns on their faces and hands.

She called 911 and asked for two ambulances to be sent to the store. Because it was so cold outside, she did not want to send them out to their car. She found some nearby chairs for each of them and thankfully sank into hers. She felt peculiar and had a fierce headache. She used her walkie-talkie to recall her Safety Team.

She unlocked the front door and let them in. They came in and were shocked to see Melissa and the older men in such a state. She asked them to make the brothers as comfortable as possible. She had no idea that her head was bleeding until the blood dripped onto her blouse. She looked at the blood in surprise. One of her Safety Team made her sit back down quietly. He was shocked at how Ms. Hillman looked. He thought that she looked about ready to faint.

When the two ambulances arrived, the paramedics first looked at the two older men. Neither of them was able to speak for the moment since they were so shocked. Melissa briefly told the paramedics what happened. They carefully put the two gentlemen into the first ambulance and drove away.

The second set of paramedics tended to Melissa. They covered the cut on her forehead with a gauze bandage and put her into a wheelchair. In their professional opinion, Melissa looked as if she was about to keel over.

As they were pushing Melissa's wheelchair toward the waiting ambulance, Erik pulled up in his car. He was a little bit early for his meeting with Melissa, but he was anxious to see her. He was shocked to see Melissa in the wheelchair, about to get into the ambulance.

He rushed over to find out what was going on. He explained who he was, and the paramedics told him what happened. Melissa had closed her eyes because of her extreme headache. She now heard Erik's voice and opened them. Perhaps it was the relief of seeing him or the pain in her head, but she could not stop herself from bursting into tears. Erik felt his heart break for her. The paramedics tried to calm her down. He looked at one of them and said quietly, "I am a good friend of hers. May I give her a hug and try to calm her?"

The paramedics thought that it might be a good idea, and they allowed Erik to come forward. He knelt on the snow-covered parking lot in front of Melissa's wheelchair. He pulled her into a comforting hug. Erik waited patiently until she stopped crying. Then he gave her his clean white handkerchief to use to mop up her face. She looked so pale and shaky that he gave her a gentle kiss. He stroked her wildly curling hair. "Are you okay?" he asked her softly. She looked at him and nodded, unable to speak just yet.

"Melissa, you need to get checked out at the hospital. Please get into the ambulance. I will follow it and wait for you in the waiting room at the hospital. Don't worry about anything, my dear. I will be there, waiting for you, when you are released," he reassured her. He nodded to the paramedic, who put her into the ambulance. Melissa rode away in the ambulance, with Erik following close behind.

Erik sat in the waiting room and waited for news about Melissa. After half an hour, her doctor came out to talk to whoever was in the waiting room. Seeing Erik, he strode over to talk with him. The doctor told Erik that Melissa was fine, with just a few cuts and tiny burns. She could be released if there was someone responsible to take care of her that night.

Erik thought quickly and told him that he was Melissa's boyfriend and would take her home and stay with her that night. The doctor nodded and said that Melissa would be released in about fifteen minutes. They shook hands and the doctor left. Erik wondered what he should do. Should he call Kay and Roy Hillman and tell them about Melissa's accident? Or would everyone forgive him if he stayed with Melissa and made sure that she was alright? He didn't have much time to do anything before the hospital released Melissa. He decided that he better call Kay.

Kay answered her phone after the first ring. "Hi, Mrs. Hillman. This is Erik Lundstrom. I am at the hospital with Melissa. There was a fire at her store today, and she was hurt—just a little. It was my day to meet with her about her food order, and I arrived at the store just as Melissa was getting into the ambulance. I talked with her briefly and followed the ambulance to the hospital. She has been here, getting checked out. There is not much wrong, just some cuts and tiny burns. They are about to release her to some responsible person. I wanted to talk with you. If you can't make it, I would be happy to go back to her apartment with her and keep an eye on her. What do you think?" he asked her.

Kay took a moment to process this information. She wanted to go to her Melly, but she was currently babysitting for Sarah Rose. Mark and Susan had a meeting for an hour or so, so they dropped Sarah off at her house. They would be back within the hour. She felt totally okay with Melissa leaving the hospital with Erik. She said to him, "Thank you for calling me, Erik. I have my granddaughter with me for another hour. If you can get Melissa safely back to her apartment, I could get there in an hour or so. Is that agreeable to you?"

That was exactly what Erik thought would happen. He said, "Yes, I will get Melissa safely back to her apartment. I'll get her comfortable and wait for you to come. I promise that I will take great care of her." His love for Melissa was evident in his voice, and Kay smiled to herself. Maybe Fate was smiling down on them, and this would be the event that got things rolling between Melissa and Erik.

Kay finished up, saying, "Thank you, Erik. I'll see you in less than two hours at Melissa's apartment." She hung up and called Roy at his work. She explained everything to him. He agreed to go to Melissa's apartment on his way home from work. When Mark and Susan arrived half an hour later to pick up their daughter, Kay told them, as well. Mark offered to go over to sit with Melissa, but his mom vetoed that suggestion. It would be worrisome for Melissa to have too many people there. Kay reiterated that she and Roy could take care of Melissa. She promised to keep them in the loop. Mark promised to call Matt and tell him what had happened.

* * *

Melissa smiled shyly at Erik. He was waiting to take her back to her apartment. It took at least another half an hour to get her the medicine for her headache and for the hospital to get Melissa to his car in a wheelchair. Apparently, that was hospital policy. Erik guided her carefully into his car and buckled her seatbelt. He told her that he had called her mother and that she would come over after Mark and Susan picked up Sarah. Melissa nodded. She still had a headache and felt very peculiar. She was happy that Erik was there. She personally felt regret that they would have to postpone their date. She supposed that they could reschedule it.

Erik saw her quietness and wondered if she felt alright. As they got to her apartment building, he asked her for her keys to the building. She looked blankly at him and then realized that she did not have her purse or keys with her. It was just too much for her, and tears started to trickle down her cheeks. He saw them and pulled her into a gentle hug. "What's wrong, Melissa?" He did not even notice that she did not have her purse with her. He hadn't given it a thought.

"I don't have my purse or my keys. They are still at the store," she confessed tearfully.

157

He just hugged her tighter and said with a half-laugh. "It's okay, Melissa. I will call your Mom. You can go to her house for the night. I will go to the store tomorrow and see if I can get your purse and keys. How is that for an idea?"

Melissa nodded with relief and used his crumpled handkerchief that she still had in her skirt pocket to dry her eyes. She wondered why she was being such a baby. Erik would probably think she was a crybaby and not want to go out with her. This thought almost made her start to cry again, but she forced the tears back with an effort. She sat quietly while Erik called Kay back and explained the new situation to her. Kay thanked him and said that she would get Melissa's old room ready for her.

Erik drew up in front of the Hillman house. He helped Melissa inside. He noticed that the smoke residue from the fire still clung to her hair and clothing, but he said nothing for fear that it would upset her more. Kay came forward to hug Melissa and take her into the living room. They both sat down and looked at Melissa. Her head ached, and she still felt on the verge of tears. Erik and Kay discussed the fire and Melissa's injuries. She had some pills for her headache.

The doctor had told Erik that she should take them every four hours if she still had a headache. There was still another hour to go before she could take them. He wanted with all his heart to sit next to Melissa, hold her hand and caress her aching head. He was smart enough to know that this was not the time nor the place. He regretfully told Kay that he would leave Melissa to her loving care.

Melissa opened her eyes wide at that news. She didn't want him to leave. Today was supposed to be their date. She wanted to find out how he felt about her. Now she might have to wait a while longer to find out. She felt in a sudden temper about that, and so she said gruffly, "I don't want to hold you up if you need to get going,

Erik." She did not look at him but looked down at her hands in her lap.

If she would have looked up, she would have seen the tender look on his face as he told her gently, "You need to take care of yourself this evening. Your mom and dad will take care of you tonight, and you will feel so much better by tomorrow. I promise that I will go to Tollie's tomorrow and see if I can get your purse. If I may, I will bring it over tomorrow afternoon." He looked at Kay inquiringly. She smiled at him and nodded her assent.

He got up to leave. He bent over Melissa and gently kissed her cheek. Melissa clutched onto his hand and wouldn't let go. He gently hugged her and kissed the top of her smoky hair. She reluctantly let go of his hand and looked up at him. Her feelings for him were plain for anyone to see. Erik saw them, and he faltered for a moment. How he wanted to stay with her! But he knew that she was vulnerable right now. She needed her mom. He knew that Kay and Roy would coddle her and cherish her all night. He hoped that he would be able to get some private time with Melissa tomorrow when he delivered her purse.

Kay walked him to the door. She studied his face. *Poor Erik,* she thought. She knew for sure that he loved her Melly. She knew that he wanted to stay with her tonight just to comfort her. Well, tomorrow Melly would be feeling better, and maybe Erik would get his chance to say something to her. She would do whatever she could to make that happen. She smiled warmly at Erik and held out her hand. He took it and looked at her. In that moment, he instantly became aware that Kay Hillman knew that he loved Melissa. He sensed that he had an ally in her. He gave her a quick grin and waved goodbye. He could hardly wait until tomorrow.

Kay led Melissa to the bathroom. She filled the bathtub with warm soapy water. Melissa was only too happy to get out of her smoky

159

clothes and take a bath. Her mom sat in the bathroom and talked with Melissa while she scrubbed herself clean. Then her mom helped her wash her hair. When Melissa was dressed in her old nightgown that she had left in her room, her mom put salve on her cuts and tiny burns.

They went into the kitchen and talked for a while, much like so many times before. Kay told Melissa she was sorry that she and Erik had to postpone their date for the night. Melissa teared up again, but Kay was quick to tell her that Erik still wanted to take her out. She told a little fib and said that Erik had mentioned it as he was leaving. Melissa felt much more hopeful after that reassurance.

When Roy came home, she had to tell the story all over again. They had a quiet evening, and Kay put Melissa to bed at ten o'clock. As she kissed her daughter goodnight, Kay silently prayed for a magical day the next day for her Melly. She really liked Erik. *He would make a lovely husband for Melly,* she thought with a happy heart. *Now it could finally be Melly's opportune time for love and happiness,* she mused.

As they were getting ready for bed, Kay told Roy everything. He nodded and smiled, confiding with her that he had his suspicions about Melissa and Erik for some time now. Kay looked at her husband with love. She hadn't known that others could see the tell-tale signs that Melissa was in love. She should have known better. Even though he rarely said anything about his children's love affairs, Roy was a deeply sensitive man. Kay hugged and kissed him and told him that he was a marvelous man. His nice blue eyes twinkled at her before he kissed her long and tenderly.

That evening Erik sat in his house and thought about Melissa. The expression on her face when they said goodbye had been very illuminating. He thought that she cared about him. *Why have we been skirting around each other for so long?* he wondered. *I've held back my affection because of Brad, but why has she kept herself behind that invisible barrier for several months?*

Whatever the issue, it now seemed as if she was finally ready to allow him to see past the barrier and reveal her feelings for him. He called his mom to tell her about the day's events. She had known that he and Melissa were going on their first date tonight and would probably call him tomorrow, anyway. Mother's intuition seemed to be at work for both Melissa and Erik.

He related the day's events to her: the fire at Tollie's, Melissa's slight injuries, transporting her to her parents' home, and sitting with her for an hour before leaving her in her parents' care. And finally, he told her about the look on Melissa's face when he said goodbye to her. Alison was so happy for Erik. She asked him what he planned to do.

He told her that he planned to go to Tollie's the next day and see if they would release Melissa's purse to him. If so, he would take it to her at her parents' home. He really did not know what would happen after that. He hoped that she would allow him to take her back to her apartment. If that happened, he would try to find out her feelings for him.

He felt like a nervous wreck. The emotional roller coaster ride he had been on appeared to be coming to an end. Still, if he had his way, they would be engaged by tomorrow night. Of course, he might have to put his hopes and dreams on hold if Melissa was not ready for his love or had some other issues that he did not currently know about.

His mom wished him the best of luck and told him to call her as soon as he could to tell her what happened. She told him fervently that she loved him. He told her that he loved her, too, and thanked her for being such a loving support for him.

He hung up and thought some more about the next day. Truth be told, he couldn't help but consider many more days beyond that. His dreams would be sweet, but it was his reality that he anticipated being much more so.

When she woke up, Melissa went to look at herself in the mirror. Her cuts and burns were not too bad. She felt presentable. She took a quick refreshing shower and put on some old clothes that she kept in her room for emergencies. Her mom and dad were sitting at the breakfast table. Dad was just finishing his breakfast before he had to leave for work. He got up and put his dirty dishes in the sink. He stopped off to kiss Kay and then came over to kiss Melissa.

"Melly, take care of yourself today. Don't rush into anything too soon. I hope that you have a wonderful day, honey," he said as he picked up his coat. She told him that she would be fine and, in kind, urged him to have a nice day as well. She waved to him as he left.

Kay asked her how she felt. Melissa had to admit that her headache was gone, and she felt fine. Her cuts hurt just a little, but otherwise, she was feeling great. Now that she was more with it, she thought about Erik's offer to retrieve her purse. She knew that the security officer would probably not release her purse to a stranger.

She asked her mom if they could go to Tollie's to see the store and to get her purse. It was about ten o'clock by now and the store should be open—or at least someone would probably be there. Kay agreed to take her. She loaned Melissa an old coat since Melissa's was still at the store with her purse.

When they arrived, they noticed that there was yellow police tape in front of the store. A security guard was stationed in front, just inside the door. Melissa and Kay walked over to see if they could get inside to get her purse. Melissa patiently explained that she was the manager of the store and had been taken away from the store in an ambulance the previous day—without her coat and purse. She further explained that she needed her purse to get the keys to open her apartment.

The security guard did not know her but realized that if this was all true, she would obviously need her purse. He called for another guard to come to the front of the store. He explained to the other guard about Melissa's request. The second guard led her to her office.

She got her coat and purse. She opened her wallet and showed him her driver's license to verify her identity.

With her situation sorted out, he felt a bit more relaxed and openly shared what he knew regarding recent updates. He told her that the store would remain closed for the time being until the Olson brothers were out of the hospital. Apparently, Thomas Olson had suffered a mild heart attack at the hospital last night. He was going to be held for several days. Timothy Olson had been admitted to the hospital overnight because he was experiencing mild symptoms related to shock and had some cuts and burns. He would be released later today if everything looked good.

Melissa was saddened at the news about her bosses' conditions and concerned for their health. She hoped that they would be okay. As she walked to her car with her mom, Melissa indicated that she wanted to make a quick trip to the hospital to see the Olson brothers. Kay said that she would be happy to accompany Melissa to the hospital and back to her apartment as well. Melissa insisted that she was fine and that her mom's help—although appreciated—was not necessary. They hugged, and Melissa told Kay that she would call her that evening and tell her about everything that happened. Kay winked at her and said that she might have some nice news to impart to them.

Melissa drove herself to the hospital. When she arrived, she was permitted to talk with Timothy. He directed her to take the next few days off work. He and Thomas would have to discuss the store's status regarding the fire damage. While he was hopeful that only the back storeroom had fire damage, until they had an insurance adjuster into the store to investigate, they could not open for business again. He told her that he would keep her in the loop. He shared that Thomas was doing well but that he could not have visitors other than family. She hugged Timothy, expressing her best wishes for both brothers, and left.

As Melissa drove herself home, she made a mental checklist of things she had to do. At the top of the list was making a call to Erik to tell him that she already had her car, purse, and keys. He would not have to make that trip to Tollie's.

At home, she made herself comfortable. She still had her Christmas tree up. She turned off all the lights except for the blue twinkle lights on the tree. The lights gave her apartment a warm and cozy feeling.

Melissa called Erik on her cell phone. When he answered, she said, "Hi, Erik, it's Melissa. I just wanted to tell you that Mom and I went to Tollie's this morning and got my purse, coat, and car. I stopped off at the hospital to see the Olsons. Timothy will be released today, but Thomas had a mild heart attack last night and won't be coming home for several days. The store will remain closed for a while, at least a week or more, so I have some time off. Timothy said he would call me and keep me in the loop. I'm at my apartment right now."

Erik was quiet for a moment but then replied, "Hi, Melissa. How are you doing this morning? Thanks for letting me know that you already have your purse. We didn't get to go on our date yesterday. How about tonight? Or is it too soon? I will let you decide." He waited for Melissa to reply as she made up her mind. It may have only been seconds, but it seemed more like minutes before she replied.

Melissa felt fine and wanted to see him. She said, "I feel fine today. It would be great if you came over. I have food in the fridge, or we could decide where to go after we relaxed for a little bit. Does that sound okay with you?"

"That sounds like a great idea. But I could bring supper with me if you would like that. We could eat it in the comfort of your apartment. Do you still have your tree up? I always like to sit in a quiet room with the Christmas tree lights on. I never take my tree down until sometime after New Year's Day." His voice was filled with the warmth of his increasing affection for her.

Melissa thought that it might be more romantic if they ate at her apartment. She said, "I like that idea. Why don't you bring over some supper? You choose—I like pizza, Italian, Chinese, or even sub sandwiches. Get whatever you want, okay? I'm not very fussy about what I will eat."

"Okay, I'll surprise you, then. I will be there at six o'clock if that suits you," he told her.

"Yes, that will be perfect. Thanks. Bye, Erik. See you at six o'clock," she said shyly.

"Bye, Melissa. See you at six," he replied and then hung up. He had to work until four o'clock. That gave him time to stop off and get her some pretty flowers and go home and change clothes before he stopped off to pick up a pizza. For some reason, pizza seemed like the perfect food for a first date.

Melissa gave her apartment a quick clean. When she was confident that everything looked nice, she turned her thoughts to what she should wear. She didn't want to be dressed too fancy for a night at home, but she wanted to wear something that made the most of her best attributes. *It's a girl's prerogative to look her best*, she mused. She finally decided on a soft fuzzy pale pink sweater and her black jeans. She decided to keep her hair loose and not put it into a ponytail. She had some delicious-smelling perfume that would add the perfect finishing touch.

Once everything was ready, she still had three hours before Erik's arrival. She would go over and talk with Brad, but he told her a few days ago that he had some late meetings all week. He wouldn't be around to talk to. She put on some music and found the novel that she had been reading. She sat back in her comfortable chair, with Clarabelle on her lap, and relaxed with her book and the music. At five-thirty, she got up and changed her clothes. She discreetly put her perfume on several pulse points and looked in the mirror. After she put on her favorite sparkling long gold earrings, she felt ready for their first date.

Erik rang her doorbell at two minutes to six o'clock. She buzzed him into the building. A few minutes later he knocked on her door. She opened it and gazed at her handsome suitor. He looked wonderful. He was wearing a light blue sweater, the exact color of his eyes. Like herself, he was wearing black jeans.

Meanwhile, Erik was enjoying his own perusal of his lovely date. The look in her eyes told him that she entirely approved of his outfit. He grinned and looked at her. She looked good enough to eat.

In one hand, he held a beautiful bouquet of flowers, and in the other hand, he held a pizza box. He handed the flowers to her with a gallant bow. Then he produced the box of pizza with a flourish. "I hope you like pepperoni and cheese pizza, Melissa. I thought that it would be a safe bet. I don't know if you like anything like anchovies or onions on your pizza."

She took the flowers into the kitchen and put them in a vase. She bent her head to take a big whiff of them. She modestly thanked him for the flowers. He grinned at her and nodded.

"I love pepperoni and cheese pizza. It's my favorite. Just for the record, I don't like either anchovies or onions on my pizza. I just like the basics on my pizza. Good choice, Erik," she said with a big smile.

They went into the kitchen and took out plates, silverware, and glasses. She pulled some soft drinks from the fridge. In the anticipation of them having pizza for dinner, she had prepared a lettuce salad to complete the meal. She took it out of the fridge and put it in some individual bowls. She also set out some croutons and several types of salad dressing. Erik placed the pizza on the table while she put everything else necessary for their meal next to it. They worked without speaking, and Melissa thought to herself, *We make a good team!*

She was surprised when Erik paused to say a blessing over their meal. It sounded natural—as if he did that every day. It was obvious to Melissa that this was not just some affectation to impress her. Wow, she hadn't even thought about Erik and religion! She considered herself to be religious, but not everyone else thought the same way as she did, so she learned to keep her beliefs to herself. She totally approved of his simple, but sincere, blessing.

They ate their salad and pizza, enjoying one another's company. At some point, they briefly talked about the fire and the Olsons. They speculated on how long it would take to get Tollie's back to normal. But soon they were discussing the fire's impact on the people who worked at the grocery store, as well as those who relied upon it as their sole source of food. As they did so, they each reached a private conclusion that the other was someone they sincerely liked.

When they were done eating, Erik insisted on helping Melissa clear up and do the dishes. She really enjoyed doing those homely little chores with him. She thought, *Of course, he's a bachelor, so he knows how to do all these things.*

With the kitchen and dishes spotless, they retired to the living room. He sat on the couch, and she sat on the flowered armchair. He felt a little disappointed because he wanted to put his arm around her while they talked. He didn't know how to ask her about her feelings, but instinctively, he knew that he would have to initiate it. She was not the type of girl who would talk like that with him. He patted the seat next to him on the couch and smiled at her.

"You're so far away, Melissa. Why don't you sit next to me? I promise not to bite you. After all, I have just eaten a big meal." Winking, he grinned at her.

She laughed shyly and acquiesced. She looked straight ahead. He said, "That's better, get comfy."

He put his arm around the top of her shoulders and gently pulled her towards him. "Thank you for letting me come over for supper, Melissa. I am really happy that we didn't have to postpone our date, again." He kissed the top of her head. She smelled delicious. He pulled her a little bit closer to him and waited for her to speak.

She turned and looked up into his face. He had a tender and gentle look on his face. She stared into his eyes. He looked steadily back at her. She said in a little rush, "I'm glad you came over; I wanted to go on this date, too."

She nervously licked her lips. He looked at them and bent over to kiss her. It was a masterful kiss, full of promises and longing. Melissa could not help herself; she felt herself kissing him back with as much pleasure as he was giving her. As the kiss went on, she put her arms around his strong shoulders. He pulled her even closer. They finally broke the kiss and stared at each other. He wanted to kiss her again, but he felt as if they should talk, first.

"Melissa, I have been wanting to kiss you like that for months, but for some reason, you hid behind an invisible barrier. What did I do wrong to make you so wary of me? I really have to know." Erik's tone was serious, and his expression was puzzled. Although this was an unwelcome break from their kissing, Melissa knew that Erik deserved to know. Still, she was tentative in her response.

"Up until I ran into Greta Brown and met Bob, I thought that you were in love with her. You were always with her, and you spent so much time with Tommy. I thought that you looked like a family," she said quietly. She had to look away from his face while she said it.

He gently turned her face to his. He lifted her chin and gazed into her eyes. "Oh, Melissa, is that why? I was never in love with Greta. I met her and felt sorry that she had to bring up Tommy on such a pittance. Her deadbeat ex-husband hadn't sent money for Tommy for a long time. Young Tommy needed someone to help him get over his shyness and awkward stage. They were just my friends. But how about you? Until a month ago, I thought that you were in love with Brad. You two always seemed so close when I saw

169

you together." Despite his best effort, frustration was evident in his voice.

She searched his face with loving eyes. Yes, she noted his frustration, but also his love. *I can't believe my eyes,* she thought incredulously. Her dreams were about to come true at last. She touched his strong jaw and let her fingers lightly caress his face.

She smiled with a truly beautiful smile as she told him, "Brad is my best friend. He was my support. He knew that I cared for you, and we both thought that you would eventually marry Greta. He was just helping me to feel better about myself." All the while she spoke to Erik, she kept looking up into his face.

Erik felt his heart race. He crushed Melissa to himself, breathing hard. With a voice trembling with emotion he finally told her, "Melissa, I fell in love with you so many months ago. I think that I loved you that first day I met you. That's probably why I was such a jerk and said those unkind words to you. I was still mad at all single women after Diane and I broke up. I was immediately attracted to you, the minute I saw you. After I had time to think clearly, I knew that I loved you. This has been the most amazing feeling that I have ever experienced. I have had lots of girlfriends in the past, but not one of them, not even Diane, made me feel the way I do, just looking at you. You are the most beautiful woman that I have ever known. When you smile, you light up the whole world."

He stopped to kiss her, again. Every heartfelt word had finally passed his lips, and now the love and passion that he felt for her was in his kiss.

Melissa started trembling and felt like crying. Erik had finally told her that he loved her. In a minute, she would say those words back to him. But for now, she would revel in this amazing kiss. She returned his kiss with all the love and passion she felt for him. They clung together for a long time. In those moments enveloped in each other's arms, it seemed that even their breathing and heartbeats were becoming as one.

When they finally broke apart, tears were falling from Melissa's eyes. Even if she wanted to, she couldn't prevent the tears from falling nor the emotions from welling up from deep inside. Erik, seeing the tears, understood. He felt those emotions, as well. He tenderly kissed the tears from her face. When he gave her a gentle kiss of understanding she tasted the saltiness of her tears on his lips. She looked tenderly at him and said, "I love you, Erik. I've known for months. I never thought that I would get to tell you. My mom and Brad have known for as long as I have. They both have been very comforting to me about all of this."

He looked at her and asked her to excuse him for a second. He stood up and appeared to be leaving her on the couch. Instead, he knelt in front of her and gently said, "Melissa Hillman, I love you with all of my heart. Will you marry me?" Erik's face conveyed an earnest kind of love that Melissa had only ever seen on the faces of two very special people in her life. In that instant she recalled every loving moment she ever witnessed between her parents.

Melissa smiled widely and nodded, "Yes, Erik. I love you, too. I would love to marry you."

With her words, Erik jumped up, put his strong loving arms around her, and swung her around. He laughed with pure delight. "You have made me the happiest man in the world," he told her.

Melissa laughed, too. She felt like she was on the most amazing ride. She didn't want to get off and resume her normal life. They would have to talk, though, and make some plans. They sat on the couch, holding hands.

Erik found out that Melissa loved children and wanted at least three babies. He grinned deeply at that. He wanted at least three babies, too. He tenderly told her about the day he had been holding baby Sarah, and Mark revealed to him that Brad was just Melissa's friend and not her boyfriend. He had felt so happy, and as he had looked down at the baby in his arms, he imagined having a baby girl just like Sarah with Melissa being her proud mother. Melissa kissed him deeply for that.

It was now December 29th. Erik asked her if she needed a long engagement, or if she would agree to marry him more quickly. She thought about her brothers' weddings. They had both pulled their weddings together in a short amount of time. She told him that it might be romantic to get married on Valentine's Day.

He personally did not want to wait that long to marry her, but setting the date was usually the bride's prerogative. He reluctantly agreed to wait until then, but really, it was only one and a half months away. He wanted her to have a white wedding, with all the trimmings. She shyly confided that she had been dreaming about her wedding day since she was a little girl. She already had some ideas about it.

As they talked into the night, they had to stop every so often and kiss each other again. Melissa remembered that just a few days ago, she had been thinking about her brothers and their wives. She wondered if the happiness that they had with their wives would ever happen for her. Now she knew that it would finally be her time to marry the love of her life. Just for that thought, she reached over and gave him a big hug. He smiled and hugged her back.

It was late when Erik reluctantly said that he should leave. He kissed Melissa passionately and then quickly got up to leave before temptation could talk him into asking her if he could stay the night. He wanted their first night together to be their wedding night. She pushed him gently out the door. They planned that he would pick her up the next morning at nine o'clock and then they would tell their families about their engagement.

After Erik got home, he decided that it was too late to call his mom. She would understand when he and Melissa told her in the morning about their engagement.

Melissa floated to bed that night. She was happier than she had ever been in her whole life. Erik loved her, and she was going to marry him. Those thoughts kept going around in her head as she finally fell asleep.

CHAPTER

FOURTEEN

Erik called in sick to work the next morning. He had so much to do today. He had never been engaged before, and he found that he was like a little boy on Christmas Day. He could hardly wait for this day to begin. Smiling widely, he got himself ready for the day. He sat down to breakfast and thought about Melissa. How he loved her! He couldn't wait to see her again. He couldn't believe that she loved him, too. While he sat there, he made a preliminary list of the things that he needed to do that day. At the top of the list was "Kiss Melissa". He grinned at his whimsy. He glanced around his home and was so happy that he had finally decorated it. He would be honored to offer this home to Melissa.

He looked down at himself. He was wearing his favorite flannel shirt, tee-shirt, and jeans. He wondered if he should have dressed up more. On the other hand, he had so much to do today. He also wanted Melissa to see the real him—this is who he was. He hadn't called his mom yet. He and Melissa needed to talk about who they would tell first about their engagement.

Melissa woke up smiling. She experienced a beautiful dream about being married to Erik. In her dream, she was playing with their children in their home. Erik came home after work, kissed her on top of her head, and then played with the children, too. After supper, he helped her put them to bed. Then he took her hand and drew her gently into his strong and loving arms. They kissed with all the love they felt for each other. She remembered the feeling that she had in her dream. It was one of deep contentment and happiness.

She got ready for her day; they had so much to do. She decided to wear her most comfortable, but attractive clothes. She thought that she looked her best in either soft pink or deep blue. Her new cobalt blue sweater was feminine and pretty. With her black jeans and silver earrings, she felt ready to face the day.

Erik arrived right on time. He presented her with a single red rose. After their first long kiss, they settled down to make their plans for the day. Erik showed her his list. Melissa laughed delightedly when she saw the first item on his list, "Kiss Melissa". *It is going to be so much fun being married to Erik,* she thought with satisfaction. She looked him over carefully. She totally approved of Erik's flannel shirt and worn jeans. She just knew that he would look that way in a flannel shirt—*my big Viking,* she thought with love. He saw her eying his shirt.

"I hope you don't mind that I'm not dressed up for today. These are my most comfortable clothes. I wanted you to know the real me," he told her quietly.

Melissa smiled and said shyly, "The first time I saw you, I thought that you looked like a Viking of old. Your hair, face, and strong muscular body reminded me of a picture that I had seen of a Viking standing on his boat looking out to sea. The way you're dressed today makes me recall that picture. I love the way you look, Erik. You have such a strong face. I love your big strong arms and muscular body. It gives me a thrill to think of being held in those arms. I used to wonder how it would feel to be held close to your body in those arms. Now I know," she broke off, blushing brightly.

Erik felt so humbled that Melissa could feel that way. He loved her occasional shyness. There was nothing he could do except sweep her into his arms and hold her close to him. He felt her tremble and pulled her even closer to him. He held her for a long minute and then kissed the top of her head.

He determinedly sat her back down in her chair. *We will get nothing done today if I don't stop hugging and kissing her,* he told himself firmly. Even so, he couldn't wait until later. When all their tasks were done, he planned to resume that most wonderful of activities—hugging and kissing on his Melissa.

They decided to share their happy news with Erik's mother first. She had been waiting for his call since last night. It would also be the quicker of the two meetings. Melissa knew that telling her parents and her brothers would take quite a lot of time.

Melissa looked up from writing on her list. Erik's gaze was fixed on her. His look of total love and tenderness made her want to cry. She smiled very sweetly at him. Her smile was the most beautiful thing that Erik had ever seen. His heart almost burst with his love for her. He grabbed her hands and held them while he continued to look at her.

Melissa noticed that his light blue eyes took on a dark hue when his emotions ran deeply. She reached over and stroked his strong lean cheek. Her soft eyes told him that she felt the same way about him. He kissed the tip of her nose and told her lightly that they had to finish their list, or nothing would get done today. She smiled at him and took her hands away from his face. He immediately missed them. With a firm determination, he made himself concentrate on the task at hand.

They decided to buy Melissa's engagement ring before anything else. That way she could show it to everyone when they made their announcement. They talked about where they would get married. He wanted her to choose. She felt very close to her own church and that community, so that was an easy choice.

He asked her if she wanted to have a huge reception in a big banquet hall. Instead, she wanted to use the St. Mary's recreation center. It wasn't glamorous, but it was the place where she and Erik had spent most of their time together. They had essentially fallen in love there. It also suited their style since neither of them was a fancy top hat and tails kind of person. Melissa was sure that Mark would be fine with them using the rec center.

Erik told her that he hoped that she would wear a white wedding gown and veil. He confessed that he had pictured her walking down the aisle with him in a beautiful white satin gown. His face was flushed with embarrassment when he told her that.

Melissa was enchanted. Her big Viking had envisioned himself walking down the aisle with her. She happily agreed that she wanted a dress like that, too. They decided that Erik would wear a dark gray suit. Since they both loved the color blue, they decided on a silver and blue color theme for the wedding decorations.

With their lists finished, they went out into the cold snowy day. Their first stop was the jewelry store. Erik had insisted that he wanted to wear a wedding ring. Melissa had wondered if he would wear one because he was such a physical man, and he used his hands so much to build and repair things.

Melissa felt a thrill whenever she looked at the lovely diamond and sapphire engagement ring that they chose together.

They called Alison Lundstrom and found that she had a day off. Her welcome into the family was everything that Melissa could have wished for. They had a late lunch together, sharing with her their plans.

"My dear, the minute Erik told me about you the first time, I knew that you would be the perfect wife for him. I have never heard him talk about anyone like that before. His love for you was already so strong, even early on. I am so happy for both of you." Alison's voice was happy and supremely content. She hugged Melissa tightly.

Melissa returned her hug. She truly liked this warm and wonderful woman. She felt so blessed that, besides her own dear mother, she would have a second wonderful mother. Melissa and Erik reluctantly left Alison's loving presence, but they still had to talk with Melissa's family. They called Kay briefly from Alison's apartment to ask her if they could come over.

Suspecting that Erik and Melissa had big news to tell them, Kay called Roy at work and asked him to come home for a few hours. When he asked why, she very happily told him that she thought that Erik and Melissa might have gotten engaged. His happy exclamation made her grin. He told her that he would be home very shortly. He said that he would bring a few bottles of champagne with him, just in case they had something to celebrate.

Roy got home before Erik and Melissa arrived. He showed Kay the fine champagne that he bought. In anticipation, they put the champagne and Kay's beautiful wine glasses in the fridge. Of course, they realized that they might be jumping the gun. Melissa could just be dating Erik. He might not have revealed his love for her yet. Still, it was exciting to imagine the best happening for their daughter.

Erik parked his car behind Roy's car. He turned to look at Melissa. "Is your father usually home at this time of the day, Melissa? Do you suppose they have an inkling about the reason we wanted to come over?"

Melissa nodded her head and said with a good-natured grin, "My mom has amazing intuition. She knew that I loved you even before I knew it myself. When we called to ask to come over, I'm sure that she somehow knew that we had exciting news to tell her. She probably called Daddy and told him to get home right away. What do you want to bet that they already have champagne in the fridge, anticipating our announcement?"

Erik laughed and gave her a quick kiss. "I'm not a betting man, love. But mostly, I think you are probably right on with your thoughts. Are you ready to go in, my sweet?"

Melissa nodded and smiled, "Let's go, Erik. I can't wait to tell them. I want to tell the whole world that we're getting married. I'm so excited about it." Her voice was soft, but her blue eyes shone with happiness.

They walked into the house, holding hands. Kay and Roy took one look at Melissa's face and rushed to hug her. Kay knew in her heart that Erik had finally come forward and told Melly that he loved her. She was happy that her mother's intuition was once again correct.

Erik and Melissa shared a few minutes of tight hugs from her parents. Melissa finally managed to say, "Mom and Dad, Erik proposed to me last night. We're getting married on Valentine's Day!"

"Oh, Melly, Dad and I are so happy for both of you," Kay told her. She turned to look at Erik and gave him a sweet smile. He saw that it was the same smile that she passed on to her daughter. "Erik, I was counting on you to finally tell Melissa that you loved her. I have known it for quite a long time—ever since Matt and Tessa's party when they announced their pregnancy."

Erik's mouth dropped open. "Mrs. Hillman, how could you possibly have known? I only realized it myself that night." He stared at Kay in amazement.

Melissa looked at him with astonishment. "Erik, that was the same night that I knew that I loved you. Isn't it extraordinary that we all realized it on the same night?" She shook her head in disbelief.

Kay just smiled calmly and said. "I know my children. I can tell when they are happy or sad. I watched the two of you together. When you looked at each other during that card game, your faces lit up. You both tried so hard not to show it, but that made your love even more apparent. Now, let's call your brothers and get them over here for a celebration. Daddy brought home some lovely champagne for us all to celebrate with."

Melissa turned and looked at Erik. She grinned impishly, showing him that she had been right about the champagne. Erik nodded and grinned back at her. While Kay called Mark and Matt, Erik and Melissa sat with Roy and showed him her engagement ring. Roy was so happy for his little princess.

Roy's easy acceptance of him made Erik happy. He missed his own father. He felt that, in time, Roy would be there for him in the same way that his father would have been. Erik looked at Kay and felt a deep affection for her. He just knew that she would get along great with his own mom.

They stayed for supper with Melissa's family. Mark and Matt both arrived with their wives and baby Sarah just before they sat down to the meal. Their hugs and handshakes were heartfelt and sincere. They were so happy for Melissa and Erik. The champagne soon disappeared as they called for several toasts to the happy couple.

Mark gently teased Melissa. "Melly, you certainly are a sly one. You had us all thinking that you didn't even like Erik. Although come to think of it, you did protest a little too much that you didn't like him. It should have tipped me off."

He said quietly, "No, seriously, Melly. You couldn't have made a better choice. Erik is a decent man. He will take care of you and love you for the rest of your lives. Congratulations, little Melly," he said as he hugged her and lovingly kissed her.

"I knew that something was up when Susan and I told you that Melissa and Brad were not dating. You looked like I had just given you the best gift ever," Mark teased Erik.

Erik just smiled at him and said, "You *did* give me the best gift ever. I would still have thought that Melissa was with Brad to this day if it wouldn't have been for your words. I will always be grateful to you for that, my friend."

Matt and Tessa hugged and kissed Melissa. Tessa put her small hand on Melissa's arm and said softly, "You're going to love being married. I can tell that Erik is really in love with you. Just think, our children will all grow up together. It's going to be so much fun."

Melissa blushed and nodded happily. She finally felt a part of the group. She remembered, not that long ago, feeling outside this group of young couples in love and having babies. She couldn't wait until she and Erik had some babies, too.

Melissa and Erik informed everyone that the wedding would be on Valentine's Day, which happily fell on a Friday this year.

It was a perfect day for a wedding. They asked Mark and Susan to be their Best Man and Maid of Honor. Tessa was so close to having her baby that Matt did not want to commit to being in the wedding. When Mark and Susan agreed to their request, they looked at each other with broad smiles. They remembered the day they had met. They were the Best Man and Maid of Honor at Paul and Sarah's wedding. It was the beginning of their amazing love for each other.

They all talked and laughed together until everyone really had to get home. Before they left, Melissa scheduled a day of shopping with Susan, Kay, and Alison. She wanted to help them buy their dresses and have them help her to find the perfect wedding dress for herself.

Erik only stayed long enough at her apartment to kiss her thoroughly and hug her tightly. He promised that he would come and see her after work the next day.

The weeks leading up to the wedding were busy. Melissa went back to work at Tollie's a week and a half after the fire, after the inspectors had made a complete investigation. Thomas and Timothy Olson were often at the store making plans and suggestions about the new and improved storeroom that they planned to have built. They were so happy to hear Melissa and Erik's news. As a wedding gift, they planned to give the happy couple a five-hundred-dollar gift certificate to spend in their store.

Looking at his brother, Thomas eagerly asked, "They have to eat, right?" Timothy readily replied, "Yes, so they may as well get their groceries from us, right?" With that, the brothers gleefully shook hands and patted each other on the back.

The night before they went shopping for their wedding finery, Melissa went to her parents' home for supper. Her father surprised her very much when he quietly declared that he hoped that his sweet princess, Melissa, would wear a tiara as part of her wedding outfit. He stated that he always thought that Melissa should get married in a tiara, like Cinderella. She had been his little princess for so many years, that it only seemed right that she dress like one for her wedding. Melissa was deeply touched by his shy request. She hugged and kissed his dear face.

"Thank you, Daddy, for saying that. I think that I would like that, too. You are so sweet," she lovingly told him. She had planned to wear her mother's veil. They looked at her veil and decided that it could easily be modified to wear with a tiara. Kay looked at Roy with so much love. He really was such a big softie when it came to Melissa. She absolutely loved that about him.

They had a successful and memorable day shopping. After finding lovely blue mothers-of-the bride dresses and hats for Kay and Alison, they found a beautiful cobalt blue silk dress for Susan to wear. Then, after searching in half a dozen stores, they found Melissa's wedding dress. It was an exquisite white satin gown with long sleeves, a very full skirt, and a tight bodice. There were just the right amount of tiny pearls and lace on it—not overly fussy or elaborate. The long train was able to be shortened by fastening it in a bustle at the back of the dress. Once they found a sweet sparkling tiara to go with it, Melissa tried everything on. Her mom cried when she saw how beautiful Melissa looked. Since the dress was a perfect fit, Melissa was able to take it home with her.

The shopping party stopped off for a wonderful late lunch. The two mothers toasted Melissa with a champagne cocktail. That day with Kay, Alison, and Susan was one of the best days that Melissa could remember. She felt so blessed to have these lovely women in her life. She took her dress home and hung it carefully in her closet. She hoped that Erik would like it as much as she did. Of course, he would not get a glimpse of it until he saw her walking down the aisle on her father's arm. She smiled as she remembered her father's sweet remarks about her being his little princess.

Late one night, two weeks before the wedding, Melissa got a call from her mom. Matt had taken Tessa to the hospital. She was in labor. Melissa pulled on some warm clothes and rushed to the hospital. She found her parents and Mark in the waiting room. Matt was with Tessa. After about an hour, Matt came out to see them. His face was lined with worry.

"Tessa is having a really hard time. She's such a small woman and the baby is a normal size. The doctors might need to take the baby by cesarean section," Matt said quietly.

Kay hugged him and said briskly, "Well, that will be fine, Matt. Thousands of women have cesareans. The doctors know what they're doing."

Matt nodded and went to talk with Roy and Mark. Melissa saw them pat his back in support. Matt went back to Tessa's room a few minutes later. Melissa and her family sat around and talked about the baby and the upcoming wedding for another two hours. It was now four o'clock in the morning. A few minutes later Matt rushed in. His face was tired but happy. The tears were falling down his flushed face.

"We have a boy! I have a son," Matt exclaimed in a humbled, and yet ecstatic, voice. He looked like he was going to fall over. The whole family surged forward and hugged him tightly. He only stayed for a minute or two before rushing back to be with his Tessa.

Kay was so delighted. Now she had a sweet little granddaughter and a new baby grandson. She was so thrilled. Her gaze fell onto

Melissa. *In a year, I might have another grandchild*, she thought with complete satisfaction.

Even though it was so late, Matt's family waited around until they were told that they could go into the nursery and see the baby. Matt was already there, his face filled with wondrous emotion, staring at his son. Tessa had finally dropped off to sleep, so he felt that he could leave her for a little while. He turned to look at his family.

"We've decided to name him Robert Roy, in honor of both of our fathers. We'll call him Robbie," Matt said proudly, looking at his father with love. Roy's face showed how honored he felt to hear his son's words. He gave Matt a fierce hug and kissed the side of his cheek. They looked at each other with respect and affection. Kay looked on and felt so blessed that her children were finally close to each other as well as Roy and her. Her life was just about perfect right now.

Everyone looked at the tiny new life in front of them. They were all humbled by the miracle of life. Robbie slept on, oblivious to the people who watched him with so much love.

At last, the family left the hospital. It was after five-thirty in the morning. Most of them had to go to work that day. They would be tired, but it had been an amazing night. Melissa tried to have a quiet day at Tollie's. Unfortunately, the Olson brothers were there, and they always wanted to talk for hours about their ideas and plans. Melissa tried not to yawn while they were talking. When she told them about baby Robbie, the brothers told her to make out a gift certificate for fifty dollars for Matt and Tessa to use at the store. Melissa was so pleased and thankful to them. *They really are dear old men*, she thought with a smile. She called Erik at lunchtime and told him about the baby. Erik promised that they could go to the hospital to see Robbie that evening.

A few days later, Erik took her to see their house. He had added a few pieces of furniture since she had last seen it before Christmas. As they wandered through the rooms, hand in hand, they talked about any changes Melissa might like to make. She liked everything the way it was. She didn't think that they needed to change anything. She teased him that she wouldn't have anything to decorate, and he knew how much she liked to do that.

"Never mind, my love. You can do all of the decorating of the baby's room when we have one," Erik promised her, looking at her tenderly.

Melissa blushed and said shyly, "I'll want your help, dear Erik. You have proven that you have really good taste when it comes to decorating the house." Erik hugged her gently for that.

She started to bring some of her things over, little by little. She put them in the spare room until she had more time to go through them and incorporate some of them in with Erik's decorations. She could see that some of her treasures would complement Erik's decor very well. Even though Erik had already decorated all the rooms, he wanted Melissa to be able to use the things she loved from her own apartment. She had such good taste and natural ability for interior decorating.

CHAPTER

FIFTEEN

The night before their wedding, Melissa and Erik had their Groom's Dinner at one of their favorite restaurants. While planning, they discovered a mutual liking for a certain steakhouse.

The others seemed to agree with the choice, for their table was rowdy and happy.

Matt and Tessa made a lightning visit with baby Robbie in tow. Everyone looked at him and saw that he had downy red hair and blue eyes. He was the perfect combination of Tessa and Matt. Before they left, Matt and Tessa made a toast to Melissa and Erik.

Melissa felt on top of the world. Her whole family was here. Erik's tender love was evident in his face when he looked at her. The champagne flowed and everyone in attendance had a lovely time. They had an early night because the wedding service was at ten o'clock the next morning.

Sarah, as Melissa's personal attendant, had gathered together quite a few people to help her decorate St. Mary's recreation hall. They transformed the rather plain wooden building into a magical blue and silver kingdom, worthy of a princess. It had been off-limits to Melissa until she would see it at the wedding reception.

Melissa spent the night before her wedding at her parents' home. Kay insisted that she serve Melissa breakfast in bed, before allowing her to start to get dressed. They sat on Melissa's bed and talked about her childhood. Kay also gave her some good advice regarding how to live harmoniously with someone. Melissa had never even shared an apartment or room with anyone and was used to doing whatever she wanted. Since Melissa had seen her parents' happy marriage her whole life, she paid attention to what her mother said.

Susan and Alison came over after breakfast to get dressed in their wedding finery. After they were dressed, Kay, Susan, and Alison helped Melissa get ready. Melissa had chosen to wear her hair loose. Her dark shiny hair curled charmingly around her pretty, heart-shaped face. With her tiara and veil and her lovely wedding dress, she really did look like a princess. Kay and Roy just looked at her, with big lumps in their throats. Their baby girl was a grown woman and would become Erik's wife today. They couldn't believe it.

Roy was so happy, even as he felt sadness. Melissa had been his little girl, his little princess. She had been the only one of their children who had stayed in contact with him and Kay through all the years. He was used to seeing her several times a week. Now, he supposed, she would come over less often. Things would be different. He would miss seeing her happy face, with its lovely smile, sitting there at his table, talking cheerfully with her mother and himself. She was so much like his beautiful Kay.

He remembered the thrill that he had felt the day she was born. After two wonderful little boys, they both had prayed to have a little girl. There was something so special about being a father to a darling little girl. Her complete confidence in his abilities always made him feel like Superman. Her belief in fairy tales and other sweet imaginings made him want to keep her safe and happy. He wanted her to keep her wide-eyed wonder her whole life. When she trustingly put her small hand in his and looked up at him with her big blue eyes and long dark curls, he wanted to give her the world. He remembered Melly looking at him seriously and asking him if she would meet her Prince Charming one day. He had assured her that she would find him and marry him when the time was right.

He knew that Erik was her Prince Charming. He hoped that Erik and Melissa would be blessed with a sweet little girl. He knew that Erik was a gentle man and would cherish his children. He looked forward to future tea parties with his granddaughters. Just the thought of them made him smile. He already had Sarah Rose. He thought then of baby Robbie; he would find the time to play with him, too.

He had not felt this emotional when Mark and Matt married their respective brides. He gently hugged his sweet Melissa and cleared his throat. It was time for them to leave to go to the church. Susan and Alison went in Susan's car. He and Kay took Melissa in their car. The weather was perfect for a February day—cool, but not cold, with a sunny sky and light clouds scudding across the blue sky.

The church was packed. Both Melissa and Erik had lived in Litton their whole life. They had so many friends who had come to see them wed. Everyone took their places. As the Wedding March started, Roy gave Melissa a last careful hug before taking her arm and slowly walking her down the aisle to her beloved. He squeezed her arm. She looked quickly at him and mouthed, "I love you, Daddy" before looking to the front of the church where Erik waited for her. She barely noticed all the guests or the decorated church. Her eyes were only on Erik.

Erik turned to look at Melissa. He felt very emotional, looking at her beauty. He couldn't believe the joy he felt in his heart when he looked at her. Today she would finally be his wife. He felt like he had waited a lifetime for her. He clasped his hands together to keep himself from shaking at the sight of her. She looked exquisite, his own perfect princess. He had not known about her tiara, but he thought it suited her very well. He had always thought that she was pretty, but now he saw that she was truly beautiful. He felt so proud and humbled at the thought that she chose him. She wanted him over every other man. He promised himself that he would cherish her all the days of his life.

The wedding service was lovely. Both Erik and Melissa said their vows with strong clear voices. The music was beautiful and uplifting. As Erik walked down the aisle with his new bride on his arm, he thanked God for his amazing blessings.

Melissa finally looked around and saw all their friends and family. Her smile was radiantly beautiful. The guests all smiled back at her, each of them thinking that she made a very lovely bride and that the groom was so strong and handsome. Together, they made a lovely couple.

A white limo took Erik and Melissa to the reception. As Erik ushered Melissa into the recreation center, he was struck by how beautifully the room was decorated. It was a perfect background for his beautiful princess bride.

Melissa's eyes filled with tears when she saw the decorations. She saw her friends and family standing there awaiting their grand entrance. She felt overwhelmed by all the love and friendship. It dawned on her that this day was not just about the love of two people for each other but also the love of family and community. It was humbling and exhilarating at the same moment.

Brad came forward to usher them inside. His eyes were very tender when he looked at his good friend, Melissa. Their relationship would change after today. Erik would be her best friend now. Brad hoped that he and Melissa would still see a lot of each other. They had gone through so many things over the last four or five years. He smiled sweetly at them both and said, "If My Lord and My Lady would come forward, I would be honored to show you to your thrones."

Melissa looked at Brad with love. He was very dear to her. She squeezed Erik's arm and said, with a gentle laugh, "Yes, of course, dear man. Lead the way."

Brad grinned and led them to two huge beautifully decorated chairs on a little stage. Sarah had convinced her helpers to erect a small temporary stage so that Erik and Melissa could sit comfortably and chat with their guests. Since there were at least a hundred guests, it would take them a long time to visit with all of them. The wedding feast would not be starting for a few hours yet, so Melissa and Erik could "hold court" with their family and friends until then.

While they sat in their "thrones", Erik introduced her to his guests, and she did the same thing for him. Occasionally, his hand would tighten on her arm and she would look up into his face. Each time, she saw his darkened blue eyes looking so tenderly at her. He wanted to get her alone so that he could kiss her with all the passion he felt for her. She looked back at him with a smile in her eyes. He knew that she could read his mind and wanted that, too.

During the wedding supper, Mark and Matt mischievously started the clinking of glasses. Erik grinned widely and grabbed Melissa. He kissed her for a long time until he heard the guests laugh and protest a bit. Melissa's cheeks were bright red by the time he finally let her go. Erik looked at Mark and Matt and raised his eyebrows at them. They both grinned wickedly. This was a ritual that each of them had previously gone through. The next round of clinking was started by Susan and Tessa, also with wicked grins on their faces. Melissa looked at them and shook her head while she grinned back at them. She remembered clinking her glass at each of their weddings, so payback was inevitable. Erik kissed Melissa's left hand and then squeezed it. He planned to save his more passionate kisses for when they would finally be alone with each other. If he had to, he would kiss her nose, the top of her head, her right hand, etc. Hopefully, the glass clinkers would soon get the message and stop.

Erik swept Melissa out on the dance floor for their first dance. They had never danced together before. He had also never told her that he didn't, or rather, *couldn't*, dance. In all his life, Erik had never learned how to waltz or slow dance. However, in the month and a half that they had been engaged, Erik had taken private dance lessons. He wanted to please Melissa.

Kay mentioned to Erik soon after the engagement announcement that the whole Hillman family loved to dance. Melissa had taken lessons while she was in high school and was an accomplished ballroom dancer. Kay and Roy had taken up ballroom dancing soon after they had gotten married. Because of his size, Erik had always felt a little clumsy. His dancing teacher showed him how to relax his body and just move to the music. It had started out being something that Erik was doing just to please Melissa, but he soon found that he had some natural rhythm, and he really started to enjoy dancing.

Erik asked the band to play a lovely waltz for the newlywed's first dance. Waltzes were the easiest dance for him at this point, so when the music started, Erik led Melissa around the floor with some confidence and style. Melissa was greatly surprised and very pleased. With Erik's personality, she didn't think that he would like to dance. He held her tenderly as he whisked her around the room. He saw her delighted smile and congratulated himself in his head for taking dancing lessons. He would have to decide whether he would tell her about the lessons.

They danced together for quite a few songs. Of course, he had to give her up so that she could dance with her father and brothers and friends. His mom was so surprised when he swept her around the room in his arms. She looked up at him and smiled softly.

"Honey, you look so much like your dad right now. He would have loved to be here on your wedding day. Did you know that he learned how to dance for our wedding, too? He had heard from my mom that I adored dancing. He hadn't done much dancing before we got married. I was so surprised at our first dance. He grinned the whole time that we danced that dance. He was so proud of himself. I was proud of him, too. After our wedding, he and I used to go dancing a few times a month before you were born. After that, it always seemed like we got too busy because we never danced much when you were a boy. Now it seems as if you followed his footsteps. I know that you didn't dance before now. You told me that a few times. I think it is great that you learned for Melissa. I'm proud of you, Erik."

Erik squeezed his mom's hands and just smiled. He had never heard that story about his dad before. He realized that they didn't talk about his dad very much. Now that he was married, he wanted his mom to be a regular visitor at their home and tell her stories to him, Melissa, and eventually, her grandchildren. Erik knew in his heart that his father was watching him from above, and he was also proud of him.

Erik and Melissa stayed until the end of the reception. They had all weekend at home together before they had to fly out for their honeymoon on Monday. They were going to spend ten days in Hawaii. The whole family planned to come over on Sunday for lunch so that they could be there when he and Melissa opened their wedding gifts.

After hugging everyone goodbye, Erik ushered his princess bride into the white limo. They drank a last glass of champagne before the driver pulled up in front of their house. Erik unlocked the front door and turned to look at his bride. He picked her up in his strong loving arms and cradled her for a few seconds. Then he walked her over the threshold of their home. He gently set her down while he closed and locked the front door. Then he picked her back up and walked her into their bedroom. He looked at her, and his dark blue eyes said that he finally would be able to kiss her with all the passion he had in his heart for her. Melissa smiled beautifully up at him, and her eyes agreed.

*   *   *